He glanced down at Amy and discovered that he'd talked her to sleep.

The sight of her there, cuddled against his chest, her long lashes resting on her chubby cheeks, cracked the wall he'd erected around his heart. And suddenly he was flooded with memories.

He clamped his eyes shut, fighting the emotions, the images of Amy at that moment, the images of them both at different intervals in the future, that horrible hope that he didn't want to have.

She isn't mine…. She isn't mine…. She isn't mine….

He took a deep breath and returned Amy to her crib, relieved that she remained asleep as he covered her.

But there was another moment when he couldn't make himself move away from her bed. When he stood there watching her sleep.

When, just for that one moment, he couldn't help wondering, what if?

What if she *was* his…?

Dear Reader,

It struck me a while ago that in a lot of families there's someone who does most of the cleanups— and not just the ones that involve dirty dishes after holiday meals. Someone who is always there to lend a helping hand.

That started me thinking, what if? (That is always where the books come from.) And this time I began to think, what if the responsible person had some really, really big life-altering catastrophe to clean up after? What if it had managed to completely rock her own world, to the point of losing everything? And what if, with no one to turn to, she was left in such a bind that she had to turn to a stranger? A stranger who had had to do some cleanup of his own because of that very same mess-maker?

That's where this story was born. And since my little town of Northbridge, Montana, seemed like a good place to take a life that needed starting over, that's where we are in *It Takes a Family*.

I hope you're as glad to be back as I am.

Happy reading!

Victoria Pade

IT TAKES A FAMILY

VICTORIA PADE

SPECIAL EDITION

Published by Silhouette Books

America's Publisher of Contemporary Romance

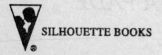

SILHOUETTE BOOKS

ISBN-13: 978-0-373-28031-5
ISBN-10:   0-373-28031-9

IT TAKES A FAMILY

Copyright © 2006 by Victoria Pade

Visit Silhouette Books at www.eHarlequin.com

Printed in U.S.A.

Books by Victoria Pade

Silhouette Special Edition

*Cowboy's Kin #923
*Baby My Baby #946
*Cowboy's Kiss #970
Mom for Hire #1057
*Cowboy's Lady #1106
*Cowboy's Love #1159
*The Cowboy's Ideal Wife #1185
*Baby Love #1249
*Cowboy's Caress #1311
*The Cowboy's Gift-Wrapped
    Bride #1365
*Cowboy's Baby #1389
*Baby Be Mine #1431
*On Pins and Needles #1443
Willow in Bloom #1490
†Her Baby Secret #1503

†Maybe My Baby #1515
†The Baby Surprise #1544
His Pretend Fiancée #1564
**Babies in the Bargain #1623
**Wedding Willies #1628
**Having the Bachelor's
    Baby #1658
The Pregnancy Project #1711
The Baby Deal #1742
**Celebrity Bachelor #1760
**Back in the Bachelor's
    Arms #1771
**It Takes a Family #1783

Silhouette Books

World's Most Eligible Bachelors
Wyoming Wrangler

Montana Mavericks:
  Wed in Whitehorn
The Marriage Bargain

The Coltons
From Boss to Bridegroom

*A Ranching Family
†Baby Times Three
**Northbridge Nuptials

VICTORIA PADE

is a native of Colorado, where she continues to live and work. Her passion—besides writing—is chocolate, which she indulges in frequently and in every form. She loves romance novels and romantic movies—the more lighthearted, the better—but she likes a good, juicy mystery now and then, too.

Chapter One

"Okay, sweetheart, we made it. We're here," Karis Pratt said.

There was no response from the back seat and Karis glanced over her shoulder at the fifteen-month-old baby girl buckled into a child carrier behind her and to her right.

It was late for Amy to be awake and Karis wouldn't have been surprised to find her niece asleep. But instead Amy was peering out the side window, her two middle fingers in her mouth, kicking her feet up and down the way she did when she was tired.

There was absolutely nothing about the scene

that should have brought tears to Karis's eyes, but there they were anyway. Hot and stinging.

She blinked hard and swallowed to keep them from falling.

"You don't know how much I don't want to do this," she told her niece. "How much I don't want to do either of the things I've come here for. If there was anything else I *could* do—"

Karis's voice cracked and she paused to clear her throat, to fight for some control.

When she had a semblance of it, she sighed and said, "But there isn't. And there's nothing else I haven't already done, or we wouldn't be here."

Here, in the middle of a snowstorm that had made visibility so slight they'd been driving for the past two hours at a snail's crawl to the place Karis's sister had called a "one-horse town, hick hole-in-the-wall."

Northbridge, Montana.

It was after nine o'clock on the last Friday of October and Karis hadn't intended to arrive so late. If she was going to show up on someone's doorstep, she thought it should probably have happened earlier in the day or evening. But she couldn't turn back time and she also couldn't risk keeping Amy with her overnight. Not when she was going to have to sleep in the car. So she resigned herself to get started on what she was dreading and unbuckled her own seat belt.

"It'll be all right," she said, unsure whether the reassurance was for herself or her niece. "This is for the best."

Karis got out of the compact sedan and peered through the snow at the red brick house she was parked in front of. It was a moderate-sized two-and-a-half-story structure with a covered front porch and big black numbers running vertically alongside the door, letting her know she had the right address. The address she'd used to answer the sole letter her sister had sent when Lea had lived here.

Karis was glad to see the buttery glow of light in the curtained front window. Hopefully that meant the man her sister had been married to for barely ten months was inside and she wouldn't be taking Amy into this cold for no reason.

She pulled her own coat close around her, smoothed her chin-length auburn hair behind her ears and went around the car.

Amy raised big, trusting blue eyes to Karis the moment the door opened and Karis felt her heart clench.

How am I going to do this…?

But just then a frigid gust of wind hit her from behind and once more the thought of spending the night in the car was all the motivation she needed. She ducked inside, pulled up the hood on Amy's coat to cover her short reddish-brown curls and to keep her tiny ears warm. Then she unfastened the seat from its moorings, and took out baby and carrier.

Karis didn't hesitate to rush for the house then. To climb the four steps to the porch. To ring the bell.

While she waited, she bent over and kissed Amy's forehead and again said, "It'll be okay. Everything will be okay."

The door opened a moment later and Karis straightened, peering through the screen at the man who stood there. Tall, broad shouldered, imposing—that was about all she could make out with the light coming from behind him.

"I'm looking for Luke Walker," she said.

"That's me," he answered with curiosity in his tone.

"I know you don't know me..."

How could he when they'd never met? But she was loath to tell him who she was. For Karis this entire trip and the two ugly errands she had to do were just added humiliations heaped on a whole pile of them that had made up the nightmare she'd found herself in the past several weeks.

But with Amy in mind, she shored up her courage and said, "I'm Karis Pratt. Lea's sister."

His first response was to reach for the edge of the door he'd just opened, as if he were going to slam it in her face.

But he didn't. Instead he kept his hand on it as his head dropped enough so, even though Karis couldn't see his eyes, she knew he'd looked down at the baby carrier she held in front of her with both hands.

He muttered an epithet under his breath that certainly wasn't welcoming, and then pushed open the screen door.

"Come in out of the cold," he commanded, as begrudging an invitation as she'd ever received.

But Karis was in no position to be particular about the amenities. She took Amy into the warmth of the entryway, moving far enough to the side of the door for Luke Walker to close it.

He turned to face her and Karis felt the faintest hint of relief. Her sister's taste had sometimes leaned toward men who could be rough around the edges, and Karis knew she would never have been able to go through with what she'd come for had that been the case with Luke Walker.

But if he had rough edges, they were nowhere to be seen. The man had runway good looks, sable-brown hair cut short and neat. A ruggedly masculine bone structure made his lean face a collection of planes and angles and sharp edges, which worked together to make a masterpiece. A slightly longish but perfectly shaped nose. A mouth that was neither too big nor too small. And eyes that were vibrant and intelligent, penetrating and piercing, discerning and disarming all at once. Teal-green eyes that were remarkably thick lashed.

And all atop a body that just wouldn't quit—shoulders and chest a mile wide, narrow waist and hips, and long, tree-trunk-mighty legs.

Karis had known he was a local police officer, which was why she'd held out hope that he might be different from Lea's other men, but this man standing steady and strong before her exuded a kind of trustworthiness that helped ease Karis's mind. Not much, but some. And some was something these days.

She bent over to set the baby carrier on the entryway floor, noting that wide-eyed Amy was surveying Luke Walker almost as intently as Karis had been.

Then she straightened, noting the dark blue uniform that told her he'd just gotten off duty. His face showed no signs of warmth; instead, he was glaring at her and steadfastly not looking at Amy.

"Why are you here?" he demanded, notably not suggesting they move any farther into his house. In fact, with his legs planted shoulder-width apart and his arms crossed over his chest, he was a towering wall-of-man, keeping her from even seeing into the living room behind him.

Karis saw no point in sugarcoating her answer. Obviously Luke Walker bore no tender feelings for her sister, and with good reason. So she said, "Six weeks ago, in Denver, there was an explosion that killed Lea, our father and the man Lea left here with."

Her sister's ex-husband offered no condolences. His only response was a slight crease that appeared between his eyebrows and a tightening of his jaw.

"It's a long story that you're probably not interested in," she went on. "But because of things that led up to that, I—" Karis stalled, choking on the words she needed to say.

But she *did* need to say them, she reminded herself. She didn't have a choice.

She swallowed hard. "I can't keep Amy. Not right now anyway or for a—"

"She isn't mine," Luke Walker said bluntly. "Even though she was born while I was married to your sister, Lea made it clear when she took off that Amy belonged to—"

"I know what she told you," Karis said, afraid that if she let him say what he wanted to before she refuted it, he might shove her out the door and never give her the chance. "I know she told you that she was leaving with Abe because Abe was really Amy's father. But Lea told me that she wasn't absolutely sure that was true. That she only said it to cut the ties with you so she could go back to Abe. And her addictions. She did things like that. But it *is* possible that you're Amy's father."

"Bull."

"I don't know whether you think Lea was lying to me or I'm lying to you, but that is what she said. If I didn't think there was any possibility you're Amy's father, I wouldn't be here. But the fact is I *do* think there's the possibility—"

"So even you're saying there's *only* a possibility."

Karis looked him square in the eye. "Yes," she admitted.

"And probably not a very good one."

Karis didn't want to acknowledge that, so instead she said, "I knew my sister. The ups and downs of her. Sometimes, if she was desperate—or determined—enough, or if she wanted to get out of something she'd gotten herself into, she'd say something that suited her purpose. But the thing is, it didn't suit any purpose to tell *me* Amy might be yours."

Okay, maybe that wasn't strictly the case. Karis had voiced her disapproval of what Lea had done and it might have caused Lea to say what she had to to defend herself, however feebly. It was just that Luke Walker was Karis's last resort, and even though she understood his doubts and didn't blame him for having them, she had to hope that for once Lea might have been telling the truth, that she *hadn't* known who Amy's father was and that he might be Luke Walker.

"But apparently it suits some purpose for you, now, to believe it," the big man guessed, making it clear he wasn't easy to put anything past.

"Look," Karis said. "Something Lea did cost me everything I had—and I mean *everything*— to keep other people, people who trusted me, from losing their business. What you see before you, the twelve dollars in my purse, the car parked in the street loaded with my clothes, and one credit card that will be maxed out after two more fill-ups of my gas tank, are all I have left in the world. I've borrowed from and imposed on friends as much as I can, but with no place to live, no job, and no references to give potential employers, I can't keep Amy with me right now. And since you're listed on her birth certificate as her father—and may *be* her father—you have to step up."

The man merely stared at her, those aqua eyes like hot lasers.

Karis continued anyway. "I think that for your own sake and for Amy's, you should have DNA tests done to find out the truth. I know that takes time and if you'll keep her *during* that time so I can just have a little while to dig myself out of this hole I'm in, then we can reevaluate the situation."

Karis had come here imagining three possible outcomes. One, of course, was that he might just flat out refuse and turn his back on Amy completely. She didn't think that needed to be said, so she only relayed her other two scenarios.

"If Amy proves not to be yours, I wouldn't expect or ask anything else of you, and I'll take her. Happily. Or maybe you'll find out she *is* yours but decide you don't want her because of Lea or because you don't want to be a single father, or whatever. Again, if I'm up and running again, I'll gladly take her to live with me and raise her and never ask another thing of you again because no matter who her father is, I love her and I want her with me and I certainly don't want Amy to ever be with anyone who—"

There were those damn tears again, filling her

eyes, cracking her voice, reducing her to something she didn't want to be reduced to in front of this guy.

"Forget it," she said, not certain where that had come from. Maybe from the last shred of dignity she had left.

She bent over to retrieve the baby, glad that somehow, even in the midst of the tension hanging thick in the air, Amy had fallen asleep and wasn't witness to this.

"Hold on," Luke Walker said then, sounding angry, annoyed and resentful, as if his back had been pushed to the wall.

Karis stopped short of picking up the car seat and straightened a second time, managing to blink away the tears once more, before they'd fallen. She raised a stubborn chin to Luke Walker and again met him eye to eye.

He didn't expand immediately on his order for her to hold on, though. Instead, he continued to stare at her, studying her, taking her measure, maybe considering what to do next.

Karis endured the silence and the scrutiny, but if he was waiting for her to beg, he had a long wait.

Then, after she'd seen his jaw clench and unclench repeatedly, he finally said, "I'll have the DNA tests done so I know once and for all if she's mine, even though I don't think she is."

"And you'll keep her in the meantime?"

There was another long silence before he shook his head. "Not without you here, too."

Karis didn't understand the edict, but rather than question it, she said, "I'm not leaving North-bridge for a few days. I have other business here."

"If it's with the rest of the Pratts, I'd tread carefully," he warned in a way that held a bit of authoritative threat to it. "But just telling me you'll be around town and only for a few days isn't enough. If I let you out of my sight you could do what, for all I know, you planned to do all along—disappear and stick me with a baby you know isn't mine."

"Amy isn't something to *stick* anyone with," Karis said angrily. "You'd be lucky to have her. Lucky if she is yours. Amy is the only right thing my sister ever did. And as for my disappearing, I'm not Lea, and leaving Amy with you in no way washes my hands of her. Even if she *is* yours and you keep her I have every intention of finding work and someplace to live that's as near to here as possible so that I can—"

Luke Walker cut her off as if nothing she said carried any weight. "There's a room with its own bath in the attic. You can use it and put Amy in her old room—the crib is still there."

"I can't do that. I have to get a job. If I stay here, too, it defeats the whole purpose—"

"I'm not keeping her without you being right here until I sort out who she belongs to. If she isn't mine—"

"Fine," Karis said before he could say more, recognizing an ultimatum when she was given one.

His eyes narrowed. "That was quick. Did I just play into your hand?"

"Are you always this suspicious of everything and everyone?" she shot back.

"Of everything and everyone who has to do with Lea," he answered without missing a beat. "I learned it the hard way."

Karis swallowed her own anger. She'd known she wouldn't be going into an ideal situation. In Lea's wake, she never did.

"My résumé is out, I'll do follow-ups on the phone from here and try to do any interviews that way, too, if I can. I can check want ads for jobs in Billings or some of the other towns or cities I saw on the road signs I passed getting here. It isn't what I had planned, but I'll make it work," she said, thinking out loud.

To give him the entire picture of why she hadn't put up more of a fight, she said, "Am I thrilled with staying in a house with a man I don't even know? No. But I need a place for Amy and if that's the only way you'll keep her, it's the only choice I have. And if you want to know the *whole* truth, staying here is better than sleeping in my car, which was what I was going to do because I can't afford a hotel room. Plus, at least if I'm here, I'll still be with Amy. I can still watch over her and go on taking care of her, and she won't wake up tomorrow morning in a strange place with only an unfamiliar face to greet her. If you call your invitation playing into my hand, then even though the thought of my staying here never occurred to me, yes, I guess you did. Want to change your mind?"

Again he didn't hurry to answer, pinning her with his gaze.

Then, with resignation, he said, "No. But I'll be watching you." He held out his hand, palm upward. "And I'll take your car keys so you can't sneak out in the middle of the night."

"How do I know you're not some kind of maniac who's going to keep me prisoner or something?" she said, reluctant to concede.

"You don't. I guess we're both having to act on some blind trust."

"You don't trust me at all," Karis countered.

"No, I don't."

He had the advantage and he knew it. And

since she'd never thought he was some kind of maniac or she wouldn't have let him anywhere near Amy, she knew his motives really were what he'd claimed—not to allow her the opportunity to take off and *stick* him with a baby that might not be his.

But that didn't mean giving him her keys wasn't galling.

"I need things from the car and the trunk and then you can have them," she said.

"Give me the keys and I'll go out with you."

Karis sighed, rolled her eyes to let him know she thought he was being ridiculous, and dropped her keys into the large hand waiting for them.

He closed his fist around them and motioned toward the door. "Ladies first."

Karis opened the door and went outside to her car. She gave Luke Walker plenty of room to unlock the driver's side door. She took Amy's diaper bag and her own purse from behind the front seat, slinging both straps over her shoulder before popping the trunk with the lever beside the seat.

Luke Walker had returned to the curb, where he watched as she took her suitcase and the cardboard box that held the remainder of Amy's things from the rear of the vehicle.

"Is that it?" he asked.

"Yes."

He closed the trunk's lid and then took the box and suitcase from her, leaving her only the diaper bag and her purse as they returned to the house.

He still didn't spare Amy so much as a glance when they got back, though. Karis picked up baby and carrier.

"Have you eaten?" he asked.

She hadn't. But something made her not want to admit it, so she said, "I'm not hungry."

He didn't pursue it; he merely headed up the staircase that rose against one wall of the entry.

Following him, Karis tried not to notice that right at eye level was a pretty fantastic derriere. This was not the time or place or person for that, she lectured herself.

When they reached the top of the steps, he motioned to his left. "The nursery," he said as if the words stuck in his throat.

He'd left it up all this time? That seemed odd, but Karis didn't say anything. She just went into the pink-and-white nursery adorned with cuddly bunny wallpaper and borders around a white crib, bureau, changing table and rocking chair.

She set Amy on the floor again as Luke Walker did the same with the suitcase and box. Then he went about putting a crib sheet on the mattress while Karis eased the sleeping infant out of her coat.

"I'll put your suitcase in your room," her surly host said, leaving her to tend to the baby alone.

Amy was barely disturbed by the diaper change or by having her pajamas put on. When that was accomplished, Karis put her niece into the crib and covered her, propping Amy's favorite toy, a stuffed elephant, in one corner of the crib so it would be within reach if the fifteen-month-old woke up and wanted it.

"Sleep tight, sweetheart," Karis whispered after kissing the baby on the forehead. Then she silently left the room, leaving the door slightly ajar.

Luke Walker was waiting in the hallway, arms again crossed over his chest.

Without saying anything he led her up a second set of stairs to the attic. It appeared to have been the room of another young girl, because daisy paper lined the wall behind the double-size brass bed.

"Sheets and blankets are clean," he said of the bedding at the foot of the bare mattress. "The armoire is empty if you want to put your stuff in it."

Karis nodded again.

"Bathroom is through there—" He pointed to

a door to the left of the cheval mirror. "Towels are in a cabinet—I'm sure you can find them. If you decide you're hungry, there's food in the fridge. The kitchen is downstairs, at the rear of the house."

Karis nodded a third time, feeling like a new inmate being instructed by the warden. Thanking him seemed inappropriate so she didn't do it.

"Do you need anything else?" he asked.

"No."

And with that Luke Walker headed for the door.

"I guess I'll see you in the morning," he said, when he reached it and turned to look at her again.

"Unless I make a run for it," she answered facetiously, not shying away from meeting his cold, hard expression.

He didn't crack a smile. Instead, he said, "Don't expect me to take care of her when she gets up."

"You won't have to," Karis said, replacing her sarcasm with defensiveness.

Apparently satisfied with her response, he turned in the doorway and went out.

Before he closed the door behind him, Karis got another glimpse of that great posterior, and admiring it just came as a reflex.

A reflex she curbed the instant she realized what she was doing.

Because regardless of the man's physical attributes, she reminded herself, they were of no interest whatsoever to her.

She'd come to Northbridge to get her life back on track and what that was going to require would not make her any friends here.

And she certainly wasn't going to enter into any other kind of relationship.

Especially not with her sister's wronged and scorned ex-husband.

Regardless of how drop-dead gorgeous he was.

Chapter Two

As he lay in bed early Saturday morning after a nearly sleepless night, Luke Walker was still coming to grips with the fact that his ex-wife had died.

He'd gone straight to the telephone when he'd left Karis Pratt in the attic the evening before. Placing a call to Cutty Grant—a member of Northbridge's police force who was on duty overnight—he'd asked for the number of the Denver police department. Then Luke had called Denver, identified himself and requested confirmation of a report that a woman named Lea Pratt or Lea Walker or Lea Pratt Walker was one of three fatalities in an explosion there six weeks ago.

Within twenty minutes he'd had the confirmation—Lea really had been killed. Her sister had told the truth to that point anyway.

And Luke had been left with one more shock to deal with when it came to Lea.

He'd wished comeuppance on her when she left him, but he'd never wished her dead. What she'd done here—to him and to the Pratts—was rotten and lowdown and lousy, but not rotten, lowdown and lousy enough for a death sentence.

He just didn't know what he was supposed to feel now. Grief? Remorse? Loss?

He'd gone through all of that when she'd taken off. All of that and so much more.

But eventually, after what had seemed like an eternity spent in an emotional pit that had felt like the deepest, darkest hallway in hell, he'd come out of it. He wasn't sure how—he guessed time had taken care of it—but little by little he'd begun to be able to look at the whole thing as one huge mistake. A lapse in his own judgment that he'd paid for—a lot.

Little by little he'd gotten over his feelings for Lea—*all* of his feelings for her. The good feelings that had gotten him into trouble in the first place, and the bad feelings Lea had left him with.

Little by little, he'd come to see that although she might have shared his house, his bed, his life for a while, he hadn't really known her at all. Who and what she actually was hadn't been revealed to him in any way until she'd walked out on him. She'd been a complete stranger. A stranger who had put on an elaborate act. A monumental ruse. A hell of a con job. But a stranger nonetheless. And only a stranger.

Which meant that now, in a way, hearing about her death was like hearing about the death of a stranger. He wasn't glad, he wasn't sad. He was just sobered, he thought, by the fact that someone he'd been involved with had come to a violent end.

And that was all there was to it for him now.

So if her sister thought the news of Lea's death was going to turn him into some kind of bleeding heart and make him an easy mark for a second attempt at passing Amy off as his, she was mistaken. No one would be more surprised than him if Amy proved to be his child. He just didn't think that was possible.

Daylight was dawning and, after glancing at the hint of sun through the window, he decided he was never going to get any sleep, so he rolled out of bed. It was anybody's guess what today would bring and he might as well shower, dress and be prepared.

But even as he went into the bathroom connected to his bedroom, Lea was still on his mind. Lea and Amy and the claim that Amy was his again.

Yes, once upon a time he'd believed what Lea Pratt had said. About everything.

He'd believed she wasn't aware that she was going twenty-six miles over the speed limit and was sorry and would slow down. He'd believed she was nothing more than the local Pratts' curious half sister who had buzzed into Northbridge to finally meet them and satisfy her curiosity. He'd believed every single thing she'd told him, including that the baby she'd delivered eight months after their whirlwind, love-at-first-sight courtship, was his premature daughter.

He'd believed it all until Lea had nearly ripped his heart out by taking away the baby he'd cared for and loved for five weeks as if she were his.

Then he and the Pratts had had their eyes opened. And faster than Lea had come into their lives, she was gone.

And so was Amy.

Luke had made it into the bathroom, but not to the shower. Lost in his thoughts, he'd stopped at the sink and was gripping the edge with both hands, elbows locked, head hanging between his shoulders as the memory of his own stupidity tormented him.

A sucker—that's what he'd been. A sucker for a pretty face, a great body and a lot of smooth lies.

He raised his head and pushed himself from the counter, making it to the shower this time and turning on the water.

A lot of smooth lies...

And now here was Lea's sister with a tale of her own. A tale of woe.

After Karis Pratt had made her announcement, Luke's first thought was that Lea wasn't dead. That she'd sent Amy with her aunt and another pack of lies to get rid of the child. That was why he'd checked up on the explosion story.

That *hadn't* been a lie. Lea *was* dead. And so was Ted Pratt. But that didn't necessarily mean anything else Karis Pratt had said was true.

True or false—not easy to tell, Luke thought as he stepped under the spray of the shower.

Hard-luck stories usually netted a bigger payoff. That was what Lea had used at the end on her half siblings. Maybe that was the angle Karis Pratt was working again.

Financially wiped out by something Lea had done.

Planning to sleep in her car in a snowstorm last night.

She loved Amy but couldn't afford to keep her....

Going over the laundry list of Karis Pratt's claims, Luke was scrubbing his head so hard it hurt.

He eased up, muttering a word his mother had washed his mouth out with soap for saying when he was eight.

It was just that it ticked him off to realize, as he mentally replayed what had happened in his entryway the previous evening, that there was a part of him that kept wondering if it *was* a scam.

But Karis Pratt had been telling the truth about Lea's death. What if she was telling the truth about everything else, too?

Damn, but he didn't want to be thinking that.

Only there were things about the night before that nagged at him. Things that might have only been clever special effects, but still he couldn't quite shake the memory.

Things like coming close to tears when she'd said she loved Amy. The *forget it* that had made it seem as if she couldn't go through with leaving the baby after all. The whole attitude— as if she'd been doing about the last thing in the world she wanted to do. Even the concession that, yes, Lea might have been lying to her when she'd said Amy was his.

She'd been very convincing.

Plus, there was Lea. Lea had taken him for a ride. She'd taken her half siblings for a ride. As far as Luke knew, she hadn't had a single compunction about lying to anyone about anything at any time. Did he doubt that she was capable of lying to her full sister, too? Or doing something that would cost Karis everything she had?

No, he didn't doubt it.

Or maybe it was easier to think that if Lea could do what she had to him and pull the wool over his eyes, she could do it to anyone.

"Or maybe you're getting taken in by another pretty face," he accused himself as he rinsed off shampoo and soap suds.

Another pretty face that was actually prettier than the one he'd fallen for before. Much prettier. Beautiful, in fact.

Yeah, there was no denying that even looking the worse for wear the previous evening, Karis Pratt was beautiful. More beautiful than Lea had been at her best.

Lea had had untamed good looks. Not trashy, but not girl-next-door, either. Long bleached-blond hair she'd artfully mussed to always appear tousled. Cat-shaped blue eyes. Lips so full they'd seemed enhanced. A chest the same way. A chest that she'd liked to show off.

But her sister? Karis Pratt had a more wholesome beauty. Shiny reddish-brown hair the color of a rain-soaked tile roof on an adobe house. Thick, smooth, healthy-looking hair that kept escaping the control she'd tried to put on it by slipping it behind her ears. Chin-length silk with bangs that teased the left brow of a face that was impossible to find a flaw in.

Creamy, alabaster skin. High cheekbones. A mouth that had some of Lea's lushness without the falsely enhanced abundance. A nose that was just the right length and more narrow, more refined than Lea's. And blue eyes that lacked the catlike shape but instead were big and round and sort of glistening, like a mountain lake at daybreak.

Karis Pratt was smaller than her sister, too. Slightly shorter—probably five foot four instead of five-five and a half. Thinner. Flatter, but still curvy enough.

Actually, as Luke turned off the shower and grabbed his towel from where it was slung over the shower door, it occurred to him that Lea had probably learned early on to overdo the makeup and hair—and even the bustline—so as not to be overshadowed by her more naturally stunning sister.

So yeah, he'd noticed Karis Pratt's looks. How could he not have? But was that making him inclined to believe her?

Hell, he *wasn't* inclined to believe her. He didn't want to believe her. He hated even wondering if anything she'd said beyond the news of Lea's death might be true.

But he *was* wondering. And if he was wondering, he knew he wasn't going to be able to just blow off everything Karis Pratt had said. Including what she'd said about Amy, and Lea's claim that she actually might be his after all.

The word he spit out then had cost him a mouth-washing at ten.

He was just so disgusted with himself for even entertaining the slightest possibility that Amy was his.

But as long as the question could be raised again, he knew it needed an answer. and it was why he'd agreed to have the testing done. And why, at the moment, Amy was asleep in the crib she'd slept in for the first five weeks of her life.

And the reason Karis Pratt was sleeping in the attic above his head? That wasn't because of the way she looked, he assured himself. Or because he was buying into the rest of her sob story.

That was so she couldn't hightail it out of Northbridge before he knew whether or not Amy was his and leave him with a baby that probably *wasn't* his.

So maybe he wasn't being conned for a second time, he told himself.

Even if the image of Karis Pratt, in all its glory, had popped into his head a hundred times during the night to remind him just how incredible looking she was.

No, this was about knowing once and for all if Amy was his own flesh and blood.

And if, in the meantime, he figured out whether the rest of Karis Pratt's story was true or false?

He'd be interested to know. But beyond general curiosity, he was definitely not investing anything in her. Not financially and not anything of himself, either.

Lea Pratt had been the most embarrassing, costly episode of his life and it would be difficult enough if he did prove to be Amy's father and ended up raising a child who shared her genes. He certainly wouldn't add a sister who shared them, too, to the mix.

At least if Amy was his, half of her genes were his. If he raised her, he could teach her to be honest and aboveboard—a good, decent, honorable person. But a full-blooded sister raised by the same people in the same environment? As far as he was concerned, that could have bred the same kind of person Lea had been, through and through.

No, thanks. He wouldn't risk it.

So while he might have to suffer Karis Pratt's temporary presence in his house and in his life, that was as far as he was willing to go. No matter how she looked.

And if she kept creeping into his mind's eye when he least expected it and didn't want it?

He'd shove her out again with thoughts of Lea. There was no repellant stronger than that.

Which meant that Luke wasn't worried about having Karis Pratt around for the time being.

Even if she was so damn beautiful that the mental image of her made wrapping the towel around his waist impossible.

Karis made sure she was up early that morning. To shower and shampoo her hair. To put on her jeans and a beige V-neck sweater she wore over a white camisole top. To dry her hair and give it the few turns of the curling iron it required to curve under on the ends. To brush on a little blush and a little mascara.

She wanted to be ready by the time Amy woke for the day.

But Amy was still sleeping when Karis had accomplished it all and so she was left waiting. She didn't leave the attic bedroom, because she wasn't eager to face Luke Walker's disdain any sooner than necessary.

As she waited, she perched on the window seat of one of two dormers that provided light and air to the slanted-ceilinged room. For the first time, she faced the second reason she'd come to Northbridge—the big, stately, brown-brick house that stood atop the hill at the end of the street.

It was two stories with a steeply pitched slate roof and a large turret that ran along one corner of both levels. A wide, covered porch wrapped the front and side of the house from the turret, shading large-paned glass windows and an oversize front door, and dropping to the sloping front yard by eight stone steps bordered by well-tended bushes.

Multiple windows lined the upper level, all of them flanked by dark shutters and fanlights above them.

It was a lovely, old house that had clearly never seen a day's neglect. The home of her father's original family.

And Karis's single, solitary asset.

Looking at the house put a knot in her

stomach, the same knot that had been forming there for the past few weeks whenever she thought about it or researched it. The same knot that formed every time she thought about how the house had come to be hers or what she was going to have to do to get it.

She had no right to it and she knew it. Just as her seven older half siblings would know it. And resent her for the way the house had come to be hers.

"Why did you have to put me in this position, Lea?" she whispered, as if her sister were there to hear.

But when it came to the house, in this, too, Karis didn't have a choice. The best she could do was vow to make the situation as painless as possible for the seven people she'd never even met.

But still, she was going to have to tell them how things stood. For Amy's sake. For her own sake. For the sake of other, innocent, trusting people who hadn't deserved what had been done to them, either.

It just didn't change the fact that in all of her fantasies of coming face-to-face with this part of her family, she had never imagined these circumstances.

"And now you're all going to hate me."

With good reason.

* * *

Amy was an even-tempered, easygoing baby. Karis always wondered if that was her nature or if it was just that she'd learned, with Lea as her mother, being demanding didn't get her anywhere.

Regardless of the reason, the baby didn't wake up fussy in the mornings. She didn't cry. She wasn't impatient to have her needs met. She merely sat in her crib and entertained herself.

Knowing that, Karis had opened the door to the attic bedroom, as soon as she was dressed, to listen for the sounds of her niece stirring. When she heard them, she abandoned her melancholy study of the Pratt family home and left her room, heading down the stairs, being careful to walk softly in case Luke Walker was still asleep.

She only made it to the third of the steps, however, before she paused in her tracks.

Luke Walker was already at Amy's bedroom door.

He was just standing there, not venturing in, only watching from a distance.

Karis couldn't see past him into the room but, from the sounds of Amy's jabbering, Karis assumed the little girl hadn't noticed him. And he didn't notice Karis, standing stalk still.

It gave her a moment to do some observing of her own.

He had already showered and dressed. Not in his uniform this morning, though. He had on a pair of time-aged, faded jeans. They fit him so well he had to have bought them years ago and broken them in. So well that her gaze was drawn inescapably to the back pockets that rode his rear in divine symphony with the tight glutes behind them.

She looked upward when she realized she was again staring at the man's butt.

He had on a stark-white long-sleeved, mock-neck T-shirt that left little to the imagination. The shirt en-cased wide shoulders, muscular torso and hard biceps every bit as appealingly as those jeans covered his lower half.

The faint scent of his cologne wafted in the air. A clean, airy cologne with citrus under-tones, the scent went right to her head and carried her away for a moment before she reminded herself that this wasn't just any man. Luke Walker wasn't simply a great-looking, single guy she'd happened to meet and might want to get acquainted with. This man already seemed disgusted with her merely by association. That disgust wasn't going to be improved when he found out the second reason she'd come to Northbridge. No matter how he looked. Or smelled. She needed not to forget that.

Even so, she couldn't help thinking that although she hadn't considered her sister capable of good taste in men, she had to acknowledge that this particular man proved Lea did have some. Either that, or she'd been uncommonly lucky.

Karis went down the remainder of the steps, making sure her footfalls announced her presence.

When Luke Walker heard her coming, those impressive shoulders drew back slightly and he took a step out of the doorway as if he'd been caught.

"Trying to see if she looks like you?" Karis asked as she joined him.

"Yes," he admitted.

"What do you think?"

"I think she looks like you—reddish hair, pale skin, button nose, big baby-blue eyes… Maybe she isn't Amy at all. Maybe she's yours and you're trumping up this whole thing to get rid of your own kid."

So today wasn't going to be any better than last night, Karis thought.

"That's definitely what I'm doing. You caught me. And here I thought you were a plain cop instead of a detective," she said sarcastically.

She went into the nursery then, to her niece, bypassing the man at the door.

"An Kras!" Amy greeted when she saw her, using her fifteen-month-old version of *Aunt Karis*.

"Good morning, sweetie."

Bringing her elephant with her, Amy stood and hung on to the crib's rail with her free hand, giving a bit of a bounce to let Karis know she wanted out.

Karis didn't hesitate to oblige, picking her up and settling the baby on her hip.

"Hi," Amy said then, spotting Luke Walker.

Karis saw that he was taken aback by the baby's acknowledgment of him.

He didn't respond immediately, though, and Karis wondered if he was going to ignore Amy. If he did, Karis's estimation of him would go rapidly downhill and she waited to see what he would do.

But after a moment he said, "Hi." And then he saved himself from Karis's blacklist by actually coming into the room.

"So…she talks?" he said, not getting too close.

"Only a few words, but she's starting to get the hang of it."

He pointed to the well-loved elephant. "What's this?" he asked Amy in a much, much more gentle tone of voice than anything he'd used with Karis.

"Eddy," Amy informed him.

"Eddy?" he repeated. "Is that your elephant's name—Eddy? Eddy the elephant?"

"I think it's just short for elephant and the best she can do with it for now," Karis supplied.

"Eddy," Amy said again, as if they were both wrong but without giving any clue as to how.

"Shall we change your diaper?" Karis asked the baby.

Amy didn't answer. She merely continued staring at Luke Walker, who stared back.

Karis let them have their moment. She knew Luke Walker was still looking for signs of himself in the small child. While she didn't know what exactly about him had Amy's rapt attention, she was at least glad to see that her niece wasn't shy the way she sometimes was around strangers.

"I wonder if she recognizes you," Karis said, thinking out loud.

"She was five weeks old the last time she saw me. I'm sure she doesn't remember."

"Probably not," Karis confirmed. "But she's usually more standoffish with strangers."

Luke Walker surprised her then by holding out his arms to Amy. "Will you come and see me?"

That was where Amy's friendliness stopped. She reared back, wrapped her free arm around Karis's neck with a vise grip, and managed to hold the elephant against her with her forearm while getting her two middle fingers to her mouth. She smacked Karis in the face with Eddy in the process.

"What did I tell you?" Luke Walker said, as if he'd proved something.

By the time Karis had found her way out from behind the elephant, he'd turned and was headed for the door again.

"Will you both eat eggs for breakfast, or does she still need baby food or something?" he asked.

Were they all going to have breakfast together?

Karis hadn't thought about meals or him providing her food. She certainly hadn't thought of him cooking for her. It seemed strange to accept his offer as if she were an honored guest when she was anything but.

"You don't have to do that. I mean, for me. But yes, Amy eats table food now—what you can get her to eat—and eggs are one of the things she likes, if you want to fix her one. If you don't, I packed some—"

"I think I can probably scramble eggs for

both of you," he said as if she were making a bigger deal out of it than was necessary.

Or was this a glimmer of hospitality or almost-congeniality that might indicate that he wasn't going to be a bear forever?

Hoping so, Karis softened her own attitude and said, "That would be nice. Thanks."

"They'll be ready shortly. Unless you want to eat them cold."

So much for hospitality or congeniality.

Still, as Karis watched him go, she realized that the idea of having breakfast with him wasn't altogether awful, and that alarmed her slightly.

He doesn't like me and he's not going to like me more when he finds out the rest, she reminded herself.

Keeping that firmly in mind, she took Amy to the changing table to put the baby in a dry diaper.

And to put Luke Walker in his place as nothing but an afterthought.

Chapter Three

"So…what do you think about Amy and I going up the hill to the Pratt house this afternoon to tell them about Dad…and Lea?" Karis ventured a short time later as she, Amy and Luke were eating the eggs, bacon, toast and juice he'd prepared for them all.

"You know their house is up the street?" Luke asked.

Since Karis had brought Amy downstairs, set her on the floor and pitched in to help, he hadn't been friendly, but he'd been marginally more amicable. Now suspicion tinged his tone again in response to her question and she was sorry to hear it.

"Lea didn't say much, but she did tell me that Northbridge was such a small place that our half siblings' house was just up the street from yours. And I found a couple of pictures in my father's things that had the house in the background," she explained. "I also know there's no soft spot for our father with the Northbridge Pratts, but I still need to tell them that he's passed away, don't you think?" Among other things.

"I suppose you do," Luke conceded. "But I wouldn't expect to be welcomed with open arms if I were you," he reminded her.

His warning didn't ease Karis's nervousness about meeting her half siblings for the first time or about having to say what she had to.

"I know that my father—"

"It isn't only him. Yeah, you're right—there aren't any soft spots for him in the family he left behind. But after Lea wiggled her way in with them and then pulled what she did the day she left—"

Oh no...

"What did Lea do?" Karis asked with unconcealed dread.

Luke paused in his eating to study her again as if looking for signs of a scam.

Then he said, "She didn't tell you?"

"I have to figure it was something bad and,

no, she didn't tell me when she did things she knew I wouldn't approve of. All she said about leaving here was that Abe wanted her back and so she packed up, told you Amy was Abe's instead of yours to make a clean break, and left you to go with him."

Luke let out a humorless sort of laugh. "Uh-huh. Well, I don't know how long she and *Abe* were planning it, but I had to go to a training session in Billings one day and while I was out of the way, she had *Abe* pack up her things, Amy's things and everything of mine that had any value—televisions, my stereo, all the video equipment, an old coin collection—"

"They cleaned you out," Karis said, getting the picture.

"*Abe* cleaned out my house and, while he did, Lea went up the hill with a story about how her poor, troubled sister Karis had been arrested for dealing drugs. Apparently Lea turned on the tears and said she was desperate for money to bail you out and retain a lawyer, and since I could only help her with part of the money, could they help, too."

Karis closed her eyes and shook her head, wishing she wasn't hearing what she was hearing.

"And they gave it to her," she concluded.

"By then the Pratts had begun to see her as

separate from your father and what he'd done, to think of her as one of the family. I even heard them talk about arranging a way to meet you, too, to bridge the gap between the two factions of Pratts."

"Lea never said anything about that."

"I'm sure. Anyway, the Pratts here are good people. They jumped in to help when Lea went to them. Each of them—and there are seven, in case you'd lost count—put in five hundred dollars. They wrote her checks that she took straight to the bank to cash. Then, while she was there, she emptied my accounts—"

"Oh, no…" This time the words actually came out.

"Oh, yes. The folks at the bank were a little uneasy with it, but she gave them the same story she'd told your half brothers and sisters. And when the bank manager tried to reach me to make sure it was okay, I was conveniently in the middle of training where no cell phones were allowed. Since I'd added Lea's name to my accounts when we got married, she had as much right as I did to access them, so the bank couldn't stop her from draining them. Then she and *Abe* hightailed it out of town, leaving me a note on the kitchen table that said Amy wasn't mine, that they'd left with the man who *had* fathered her. They were long gone by the time I learned how she'd spent the day. I guess she gets merits for organization and quick work."

"I'm sorry," Karis said feebly.

Luke Walker didn't respond.

"And I've never had anything to do with drugs or been arrested or—"

"I know. When I realized what she'd done I did some checking that I regretted not doing earlier. On you both. I saw that you didn't have any arrests or charges against you. But Lea had an extensive record—drug possession, selling drugs, petty theft, burglary—"

"She had a lot of problems," Karis said, glancing in Amy's direction.

The baby was sitting in a high chair that Luke had brought up from the basement and set at the round kitchen table. She was picking up pieces of scrambled egg with her chubby fingers and feeding herself directly from the tray.

Of course she was oblivious to what was being said about her mother, but Karis was uncomfortable getting into too much detail about Lea with Amy in earshot. Irrational though it might have been, it just didn't seem right.

She tried to make sure the tiny child was distracted by breaking up a slice of toast into small bites and adding that to the eggs before looking at Luke again.

"I'm sorry," she repeated. "I really am."

"Did you have something to do with it?"

"No! I'm just sorry that Lea did what she did. To you. To them. To everyone."

Those blue-green eyes of his were still focused on her and Karis felt like a bug under a microscope. But she opted to ignore it and deal with the other matters at hand.

"I can see why the real Pratts aren't going to be happy to have me show up after that," she said. They would likely see her having ownership of their house in an even worse light, if that were possible.

The thought made her all the more loath to go through with her second errand in Northbridge and she realized that, at the very least, she wasn't going to be able to rush anything to do with the house. She was going to have to find the most diplomatic way of handling it.

But in the meantime she also knew she still had to tell them about their father's death.

"I really don't want to go up there now," she said quietly.

Luke didn't say anything for a while. He just went on scrutinizing her.

Then, as if his better nature had to prevail

whether he liked it or not, he said, "Do you want me to go with you?"

The offer surprised her.

"Would you do that?"

Not happily—if the somber expression on his handsome face was any indication.

But after another moment, he said, "Yeah, I'd do that."

"It would really help not to have to go alone," she said, meaning it and appreciating any support when she was feeling so unsure of herself.

"I'll call first. Not all of them live in the house anymore, but I'll make sure they get everyone to be there for this."

"Thank you," Karis said with a full measure of her gratitude in her voice.

And while the other Pratts might not have a soft spot for their father, and certainly couldn't have one for Lea, either, a soft spot in Karis's heart began to open up at that moment.

For Luke Walker, for the kindness he was showing her.

Even if that kindness was reluctant.

It was late that afternoon before all the Pratts could gather at the house up the street to see Karis.

The snow had stopped falling before dawn and the sun had remained shining through the day, melting what had accumulated on the streets and sidewalks but leaving a white blanket on the grassy areas. The temperature was comfortable, so Karis bundled up Amy and carried the baby with her as she and Luke walked to meet with her half siblings.

Karis didn't say anything along the way. She was too nervous. But she was still glad to have the big man by her side.

He rang the doorbell when they reached the house and held the screen for her when the door was answered by a large man who was dressed in the same police uniform Luke had had on the night before.

"Hey, Cam," Luke greeted him.

"Luke," the other man responded, stepping aside for Karis and Luke to come in but never taking his eyes off Karis. Eyes that were every bit as suspicious of her as Luke's had been, and no more welcoming.

"This is Karis. Karis, this is Cam."

"Hi," Karis said, thinking that in all of the awkward situations she'd found herself in recently, this had to be the worst.

"And is this Amy?" Cam Pratt asked.

Karis hadn't thought about the fact that this man and the rest of her half siblings already knew Amy from the five weeks after her birth, but that question and the familiarity in his voice brought it home for her.

"That's Amy," Luke confirmed when Karis was slow in answering.

Cam nodded, taking a concentrated look at the infant but not making any overtures toward her.

"We're all in the living room," he said, leading the way from the vast Victorian-style entry that boasted a pedestal table in the center and a wide staircase rising from just beyond it to curve to the second level.

Luke waited for Karis to follow Cam, bringing up the rear.

The living room was large and, because it was furnished in a country motif, it lacked the formality of the entry. It was warm and welcoming, unlike the faces of the other people in the room.

"Hi," Karis said quietly to everyone.

"Sit down," one of the two women invited, pointing to the vacant love seat at a right angle to the couch.

Karis did, sitting only on the edge of the cushion and placing Amy on her lap.

It didn't seem that she should take Amy's coat completely off as if they were going to stay for a leisurely visit, but it was too warm to keep the baby bundled up. So Karis smoothed the hood back, fluffed Amy's reddish-brown cap of curls and unzipped the coat, leaving it open but on.

"Is this Amy?" the other woman on the couch asked, echoing her brother's question.

"It is." Karis answered without hesitation this time.

She had the sense that had this been fourteen months ago the woman would have tried to hold Amy or play with her. But as it was, everyone kept their distance.

Luke had remained standing beside the love seat rather than sit with Karis and Amy so he made the introductions from there.

"You met Cam at the door," he began, addressing Karis. "That's Mara, Neily and Scott on the sofa—"

"I'm Mara," said the woman who had asked about Amy. "This is Neily," she added with a glance at the woman who had invited Karis to sit.

Karis said another, "Hi."

"Boone and Jon are by the fireplace," Luke continued. "Taylor is in the chair. Boone, Taylor and Jon are the triplets—in case you didn't notice that they look almost exactly alike."

Karis nodded.

"And this is Karis," Luke finished unnecessarily.

No one seemed to know what to say, and

Karis wasn't sure whether to merely blurt out what she'd come to tell them or try to find some way to ease into it.

It was Cam who broke the silence before she'd decided. "What can we do for you?"

Clearly they were all leery of her and her motives for being there, so Karis opted for getting to the point.

"I'm afraid I have some bad news."

As she said that, she wondered for the first time if they would consider the news bad. Maybe they wouldn't.

"I needed to tell you all that Dad…"

She stalled. Somehow referring to him like that seemed proprietary and she was afraid his first family would take offense.

"That your dad…"

But he *was* her father, too, so that was weird.

"Well, your dad and mine…"

No, that wasn't good, either…

"It's okay," Luke said in a calming voice. "Just tell them."

Grateful to him once more—this time for the steadying influence—Karis swallowed and took his advice. "There was an explosion in Denver six weeks ago. Dad…and Lea…were killed."

The response of the other Pratts varied, but none were too overt. Some eyebrows rose. Some mouths gaped slightly. Some faces paled. No one appeared unaffected or as if they were glad to hear it, but there weren't any tears, either.

Again, after a few moments of silent shock, it was Cam who spoke. "What happened?"

Karis took a measured breath and said, "Lea had done something that caused a lot of problems for a lot of people—"

"Isn't that hard to believe," Boone, one of the triplets, said sarcastically under his breath.

His tone made Karis even more uncomfortable, but she didn't show it. She recognized that he had a right to think badly of Lea and thought that maybe she should let them know she was aware of her sister's misdeeds.

"Luke told me this morning what Lea did the day she left here, so I know none of you think much of her—"

Once more, Karis paused to consider what she was going to say. She didn't want any of the people in the room to think worse of her sister than they already did. In fact, it suddenly seemed important for them to understand Lea, if only a little.

So rather than rushing into telling them more about the explosion that had taken lives, she said, "I'm sorry for what Lea did to you. I know that probably doesn't mean much but if you really knew Lea, you'd know how truly messed up she was. She had drug problems from the time she was a teenager. She'd clean up her act for a while and be great—personable and sweet and fun and kind and…"

Karis's eyes welled up at the memory of her sister. She didn't want to break down, though, so she fought not to and went on.

"I think that was the Lea you all met. And knew while she was here. While she was pregnant. The clean and sober Lea. The Lea I always hoped would prevail. The trouble was, that just never seemed to happen. She couldn't stay off the drugs and when she was doing them…" Karis shrugged helplessly. "Well, she wasn't that same person."

Karis could see in the expressions of her half siblings that there still wasn't much sympathy for her sister, so she gave up trying to elicit any and forged ahead.

"Abe—the man Lea left Luke for—" Karis gave Luke an apologetic glance over her shoulder before focusing on everyone else again. "Abe had his own drug problems, but when they got back to Denver they both swore they were staying clean. For Amy's sake. I believed them and, from everything I saw, they actually were sober until about a month before the explosion.

I'd gotten Lea a job and she had been coming to work every day, not doing anything that alarmed me." Although Karis knew now that she'd been naive. "But that month before, Abe lost his job," she said. "And that must have been when things started to break down again."

Karis didn't want to get into much about how the general breakdown had affected her own situation, so she cut to the chase.

"Like I said, Lea had done something that affected a lot of people and Dad went looking for her. I say *looking for her* because when he went to where she and Abe *had* been living, he found out they'd been evicted a week earlier— which I didn't know, either, but it made sense because Lea had asked if Amy could stay with me for a few days right around the same time. Luckily Amy was still with me when Dad found Lea and Abe."

Karis hadn't realized it, but she'd been hugging Amy and apparently her grip on the baby was too tight, because Amy began to squirm.

Karis loosened her hold and kissed the crown of Amy's head as compensation.

Then she went on. "Dad found Lea and Abe living in a mobile home out in the middle of nowhere. Lea, Abe and another man. But they weren't only living in the trailer, they were also making methamphetamine there, to use themselves and to sell on the street. When Dad showed up, the other man went outside rather than be in the middle of a family fight. He could hear and see what was going on inside, though, and according to him, Dad and Lea argued and then Abe got into it, too. It became physical—"

Amy was getting antsy and Karis took a cracker from a sandwich bag she had in her pocket and gave it to the baby.

She took a deep breath and continued. "I don't know anything about the setup of a meth lab, but apparently it's volatile and dangerous. In the struggle between Dad and Abe, something happened that caused the explosion. The man outside was thrown and hurt, but he lived to tell what happened. Dad, Lea and Abe were all killed."

Another moment's silence fell and Karis let her final statement stand alone.

Then, as if he were doing an interrogation, Cam said, "And you say this all happened six weeks ago?"

"Yes."

"But you're just now getting around to letting us know?" Cam said.

"There were so many complications and problems that I was left with," Karis said, still not wanting to get into everything at the moment. "I'm sorry, but I didn't think you should be told over the telephone by someone you'd never even met. I thought you all deserved to hear it in person, but this is the first I could get away."

"Was there a funeral?" Mara asked quietly but also with a note of insult that there might have been and they hadn't been invited.

"No," Karis was quick to tell her. "This isn't pretty and I'm sorry to have to say it, but the explosion caused an inferno in the trailer. There were no remains—"

"That's a little convenient," Cam said under his breath.

Obviously he thought she was trying to pull something.

But before Karis could respond, Luke said, "I called the Denver police for verification. She's telling the truth about the explosion and about the aftermath. Because the trailer was far from any fire station—or anything else for that matter—by the time the explosion and fire were called in and firefighters arrived, there was nothing but ash and the injured man to tell the story. Forensics sifted through the rubble and found enough in the way of gold tooth fillings, some other dental work, and a few bone fragments, to confirm that your father and Lea were killed."

"So there wasn't anything *to* bury," Neily concluded with a grimace.

"And I couldn't arrange a memorial service," Karis said. "There just wasn't…a way," she finished, faltering to keep from saying there hadn't been money for any kind of service, along with the fact that she'd been left in such a predicament that she hadn't been able to do anything but try to dig out of it.

Then, again thinking of their feelings, she said, "Of course, if you want to have something—"

"Is that why you're here?" Cam asked, cutting her off. "So we'll do something or give you the money to do something?"

He definitely thought she had an angle.

"No," Karis said. "I only meant that if it would make you all feel better to have some sort of service—"

"It's tough to mourn somebody you didn't know," another of the triplets—Taylor—said.

Karis nodded again. "I didn't really think you'd want to have any kind of memorial or anything. I just thought you all should know what had happened."

"That's the only thing you came for?" Cam asked. "Just to tell us?"

Karis didn't want to lie to them and then, in a day or two, let them know that wasn't the only thing she'd come for, that she also owned their house and needed to use it to get herself the rest of the way out of the trouble Lea had left her in. But she also knew this was not the time to get into the other reason she'd come to Northbridge. So rather than give a direct answer, she decided it was best to get in and get out. She'd gotten in, told them the first half of what she'd come to tell them, and now it was time to get out before she actually did say anything more.

"I'm sorry to be the bearer of bad news," she said, letting no answer be her answer as she pulled Amy's hood up and rezipped the baby's coat. "And after what Lea did here, I don't blame you for being suspicious. But now that you know what happened, I'll leave you to…digest it, I guess. Again, I'm sorry," she added as she stood.

She was going to have that be the end of it. Then it struck her that she didn't want to leave them thinking what they—particularly Cam— seemed to think of her.

She paused and said, "I know you all probably won't believe this, but Lea and I were always different. *Very* different. Not that I didn't love her, because I did. Even when I hated what she was doing, I still loved her and the person she was when she wasn't on drugs. But among people who knew us both, no one would ever put me in the same category as my sister, and I'd really appreciate it if you could find a way to separate us in your minds, too. To maybe reserve judgment a little."

No one said anything and Karis decided her exit was going to be just as awkward as the rest of the visit, and nothing would change that. She turned to go.

As she did, a cheery Amy swiveled in her arms to look over her shoulder and call, "Bye-see-ya-guys."

A small ripple of involuntary laughter came in response.

Even Karis couldn't help smiling.

But since none of the other Pratts said anything to halt their retreat, Karis took Amy back into the entryway and out the front door.

Bolstered more than he could know by the fact that Luke Walker had come with her.

Chapter Four

"Going somewhere?"

Karis considered it just her luck for Luke to drive up at the very minute she was attempting to break into her own car.

"I was hoping I'd left a door unlocked so I could pop the trunk from the inside," she said truthfully.

His only response was to roll up his window and go the rest of the way to the driveway.

He'd been called into work for an impromptu meeting when they'd arrived back at his house after visiting the Pratts that afternoon. He'd left Karis alone with Amy and with no clue when he'd return.

Not only had he scrambled eggs for their breakfast, he'd also made sandwiches for them all for lunch—again with Karis making it clear that he didn't need to provide her meals and him ignoring it. But the dinner hour had come and gone, and since she didn't feel comfortable raiding his cupboards or refrigerator, she'd dug into the food supplies she'd packed with Amy's things and fixed the baby an individual serving of macaroni and cheese and opened a toddler-size jar of plums.

Karis hadn't eaten anything then, but that had been over two hours ago and as it drew near eight o'clock she was hungry herself. And, in response to the stress of the day, she was also craving chocolate like crazy. Which was why she'd decided to see if she could get into her own stockpile of foodstuff in the trunk.

Once he'd parked, Luke got out of his SUV and joined her where she waited on the sidewalk beside her car.

"You need something out of the trunk?" he said.

"Food."

"You have food in the trunk?"

"Some canned goods, some crackers and peanut butter, some stuff I could microwave at a convenience store." And chocolate.

"Field rations for living in your car?"

"Yes."

He held up a fast-food bag she hadn't noticed. "How about burgers instead?"

"How about burgers first and then a chocolate bar?" she countered enticingly, nodding toward the sedan.

"You only have twelve dollars to your name, you were going to sleep in your car and eat out of your trunk, but you brought chocolate?"

"That's my addiction," she confessed.

He shook his head as if the idea was lost on him. But he reached into his jean pocket, produced her keys and opened the trunk.

Karis wasted no time dragging the box of food to the front and retrieving the bag of miniature chocolate bars she'd hoped she could make last longer than full-size bars it would have been impossible to eat only portions of. Then it occurred to her that if she didn't want to eat her host's food, she needed her own and she picked up the box.

"Is the whole thing full of chocolate?" he asked.

"No, but I feel funny eating your food."

"We'll trade food for services, if it'll make you feel better. Just bring your chocolate and leave your field rations."

Services?

She didn't know much about the man but she knew he wasn't alluding to sexual services. So why did *she* have sex on the brain the minute he'd said that?

She curbed it in a hurry, replaced the box in the trunk and, as he closed it, said, "What kind of services?"

"Tomorrow we'll hit the store, and I'll buy some groceries. You can cook and do the cleanup. Can you cook?"

"Pretty well, actually."

"Great. It's not my favorite thing. And maybe vacuum or dust or something, too."

As long as she didn't have to clean his bathroom, that seemed like a fair trade.

"Deal," she said, even though he was already headed for the house and hadn't waited for her agreement.

Karis followed him, watching the play of bodacious butt behind denim and again she had to pull her thoughts into line.

What am I doing? she asked herself, wondering if her subconscious was on a quest for another kind of stress relief.

"I bought Amy a burger, too," Luke said, as she closed the door and he took off his coat to hang on the hall tree.

Karis had to work at recalling what he was talking about.

Amy...

Burgers...

"Too late," she answered when she'd put two and two together. "Amy ate, had a bath and is sound asleep."

"What did you feed her—leaves and berries you foraged in the backyard?"

As they went to the kitchen, Karis explained that she'd supplied Amy with some field rations, too, and that was what the baby had eaten.

"I don't know how you were raised," he said when she'd finished, "but in a Walker house, food is never off-limits to anybody, whether they were invited, not invited, expected or un-expected. From now on, just help yourself, whether it's for you or for Amy."

It still didn't seem quite right, but Karis thought that if she could do a chore here and there it might make her feel as if things were evened out a little.

"You can start to earn your keep by getting us a couple of sodas," Luke said then.

Karis wasn't sure, but there almost seemed to be an edge of humor to his tone. Was it possible that he was going to lighten up? She might even consider cleaning his bachelor bathroom to ac-complish that.

She took two cans of cola out of his refrigerator and brought them to the table where he was setting out burgers and fries.

Deciding to test the water and see if they might actually be able to have a normal conversation, she said, "Was your meeting some kind of emergency?"

"No, no emergency," he answered as they sat down to eat. "We're in the process of opening a new investigation of an old case. The state police consented to send in a search team to help us, but they weren't supposed to be here until Monday. For some reason they showed up this afternoon to work through the weekend. Everyone had to be briefed and updated and shown around—that kind of thing."

He'd offered that information civilly and it encouraged Karis to ask more.

"What are you searching for?"

"The body of a man who robbed the bank in 1960."

"He robbed the bank and died and you just started looking for him?"

Luke had taken a bite of his hamburger and, while he chewed and swallowed, he shook his head. "Two men—itinerant farm hands— robbed the bank. Until a few weeks ago we thought they'd both gotten away with it. And with the wife of the man who was our Reverend at the time—"

"Ooh, a little soap opera."

"Afraid so. It seems the Reverend's wife got restless and hooked up with one of these two guys, purportedly not knowing that they had any intention of pulling a bank job. But once they had, it looked as if the Reverend's wife and the robbers had gotten away."

"But they hadn't?"

"The town is named for an old bridge that's being refurbished. In the process, one of the workmen came across a duffel bag in the rafters. Inside the duffel bag were the belongings of one of the men and there were bloodstains on the outside of it, which prompted our looking into things again. When we did, we discovered that the FBI—which has jurisdiction in bank robberies— had actually caught one of the robbers, the one the Reverend's wife was involved with. He'd claimed that the Reverend's wife didn't know ahead of time that they were going to pull the bank job, and the other robber had taken his share of the money and gone his separate way. But since there was never another sign of the second robber—"

"And now that you've found the second robber's bloodstained duffel bag…" Karis said, to let him know she was paying attention.

"Right, and now that we've found the second robber's bloodstained duffel bag, we're thinking that the guy didn't make it out of Northbridge, that the first robber killed him and buried him rather than split the money."

"And then took off with the Reverend's wife," Karis added. She wasn't really invested in the story, but she was so happy that Luke was in a better mood that she wanted to encourage it.

"And then took off with the Reverend's wife," he repeated. "But she wasn't with the first robber when the FBI caught up with him. During questioning, he told the agent that she'd been distraught over leaving her two sons back here with her husband. She'd been upset all the time, crying, overeating—which was making her less attractive to him—and she'd just all-round become not much fun. So he snuck out in the middle of the night and left her on her own in Alaska."

"Ouch!" Karis said with a grimace.

"The robber the FBI caught was shot to death during an escape attempt and that's where the investigation stopped. Because of personnel changes with the feds and here in town, because there was no trail at all on the second robber, and because no one believed the Reverend's wife had had anything to do with the robbery, the whole case got put on a back burner and eventually forgotten about. But now that it looks as if the second robber might have been killed, we're looking for his body. If we find it, that opens a whole new can of worms."

"Then it's a murder case and not just a bank robbery."

"And while the feds were content to take the robber's word that the Reverend's wife, Celeste Perry, wasn't involved in the bank job, the murder of the second man before she and her boyfriend left town could put a different spin on her role in everything. She could either have been a witness to or a participant in a murder. Plus, even though she'd be of retirement age now, it's reasonable to think she might still be alive and, since entries on the last report all agree that she was determined to get back to Northbridge at some point, this whole thing needs to be pursued."

"Not only a soap opera but a mystery and a scandal for a preacher, too—the plot thickens," Karis said.

"It seems to be, yeah."

"And here I thought this was a small, quiet town like in the movies and on TV."

"As a rule, it is," Luke said.

"But now you get to stretch your cop

muscles. Are you glad for the stimulation or sorry to have the norm disturbed?"

"Both," he admitted. "On the one hand it's a little exciting. On the other hand none of us are eager to stir up dirt for the Reverend and his sons and grandchildren. And there could be a lot stirred up if we find a body."

"And the search is on."

"Beginning tomorrow it is."

"Will you be doing it?" Karis asked.

"Some of it. The state guys will focus only on that. There's a lot of wooded area around the bridge where the duffel bag was found. As for the local cops, we're such a small force we don't have the manpower to assign anyone to work the search and only the search, so we'll each just pitch in during our regular shifts as long as things in town stay quiet, which they usually do. We have the option of working it during our off hours, too, but I told them at the meeting today that I have my hands full with other things."

"Me and Amy."

"You and Amy," he said, leveling green eyes on her.

But they didn't seem as hard or as cold as they had before and it was such an improvement that Karis didn't mind it this time.

Then he broke the connection and, seeing that she'd finished her burger, offered her a second one.

When she turned it down, he unwrapped it for himself. After the initial bite, he said, "Speaking of which—"

"Of me and Amy?"

"Of *me* and Amy," he amended. "I've set up the blood draws for the DNA test. We'll go in tomorrow."

"On a Sunday? I didn't think anything would be done until Monday."

"One of my brothers is Northbridge's doctor. He doesn't have an office. When the town anted up for the small hospital the community needed, we did away with the doctor's office and placed all the medical care in the hospital. Mainly out of the emergency room. Anyway, Reid will meet us there tomorrow. Getting it done on a Sunday is a perk of having a doctor in the family. Results will take at least six weeks, so I want to get the process started as soon as possible."

Karis nodded, wondering if that meant he expected her to stay in Northbridge for six weeks.

Not that she had anywhere else to be, because she didn't. But she doubted anyone would be too thrilled with her still being around once she revealed information about her inheritance.

But now wasn't the time to bring that up.

When Luke had polished off his second hamburger and the rest of the fries, Karis proved she was willing to earn her keep and gathered everything to throw away.

Because things between them had been amiable to that point, she ventured another question—this one more treacherous because it brought up her sister again.

"By any chance, did Lea leave anything of hers behind when she moved out?"

Karis was washing off the table by then and although she wasn't looking at Luke, she could feel the atmosphere chill at the mere mention of her sister's name.

"She left a few things. Why?"

"Our mother had a locket that she gave me just before she died. It was special to her—and to me—and Lea borrowed it and never returned it. I asked for it back when she got to Denver again, but she said she couldn't find it, that she must have left it here. I just wondered if she might have."

"As opposed to having pawned it for money to buy drugs?"

"I just wondered if it was here," Karis reiterated, rather than adding to the list of indictments against Lea.

"I don't remember a locket, but I kept what she left in case she wanted any of it back. You're welcome to it."

"Could I go through it now, or is it put away somewhere that's a pain to get to?"

"It's just in the top of the linen closet upstairs. I'll be glad to have the shelf space cleared. I'll go get it."

"Do you need help?"

"I think I can handle it. I'll meet you in the living room."

Karis rinsed the sponge she'd been using and by the time she got to the living room, Luke was coming down the stairs carrying a cardboard box.

He set it on the claw-foot, oval coffee table and then sat in the oversize gray tweed armchair angled to one side of the matching sofa.

"This is it?" she asked, despite the fact that it obviously was.

"This is it."

Karis peered into the box, then sat in the center of the couch and pulled the box toward her to go through it.

Most of what was inside were Amy's things—newborn clothes and booties, a tiny stuffed duck, a rattle, a pacifier and a bottle.

Karis took the items out and piled them on

the coffee table to one side of the box. Then she began to pull out her sister's things.

There was a blush compact that was mostly used. A lipstick. A comb. A sock with no mate. A tank top. A fashion magazine.

Once most items had been placed on the table, there remained only an old shoe box.

"If the locket is anywhere, it would be in there. That's where she kept small things," Luke informed her. "I went through this stuff when she left. I don't remember a locket but maybe I missed it."

Karis took the box out and placed it in her lap, opening the lid.

An expired driver's license was the first item that caught Karis's attention, probably because Lea's picture was faceup for her to see.

Blond hair that fell to the middle of her back in a thick curtain that Karis had always been jealous of. Eyes not quite as blue as Karis's. A slightly bigger nose. A smile that came easily, naturally, and never with any self-consciousness or inhibition. A winning smile that had gotten Lea out of many scrapes. And probably into Luke's life.

Seeing that photograph gave Karis a twinge and made her think, as she had many times before, that Lea hadn't had to end up the way she had, that she'd had the potential for so much more.

Karis set the license aside and searched through the rest of the contents of the shoe box.

Nail file and polish. Eyeliner. A tube of hand lotion. And a man's wallet. A wallet Karis recognized.

"No locket?" Luke asked.

"No," Karis confirmed sadly, hoping he was wrong in thinking that her sister had pawned their mother's sole piece of cherished jewelry rather than simply misplacing it.

She did take out what she had found, though, focusing her attention on the wallet as she ran her thumb over the initials embossed in the leather.

"There's no identification in it," Luke said when he saw it. "I found it in the back of one of her drawers and put it in the shoe box when I was packing things up."

"It belonged to our father. I gave it to him for his birthday two years ago. He thought..." Or at least that was what he'd told Karis. "He thought he'd lost it."

"But Lea *borrowed* it, too?"

"Abe could have stolen it. That was more his line. Or pushing Lea to take things."

"Is that how you excuse everything your sister did—*Abe* made her do it?"

"I'm not saying Lea was innocent, just that without Abe's urging or planning or prodding or pressuring there are a lot of things I don't think she would have done."

Luke stared at her for a moment as if sizing up her gullibility. Then, clearly not holding the same point of view, he said, "And that allows you to think better of your sister."

Karis shrugged and looked at him rather than at the wallet she was holding. "Given your feelings about Lea, I keep wondering why you didn't chase her down and have the book thrown at her, legally, when she left here."

"I couldn't," he said. "Emptying joint bank accounts isn't a criminal act. Neither is a wife leaving her husband and taking the television. I could have gone through civil court to try to recoup some of what she'd helped herself to, but once I saw her police record and got a clear picture of the kind of person she really was, I knew it would only be a waste of my time and more of my money on attorney fees. The Pratts could have pressed charges, but they opted not to."

"Why?"

"A couple of reasons. Like anyone who gets swindled, they were embarrassed at having trusted Lea, at falling for her lies and handing over their money so freely in what was nothing but a con job. They also decided that doing it might somehow bring your father into the picture, too—in defense of her, maybe—and they didn't want that. They said nothing was worth having to ever lay eyes on him again."

"They're bitter on that score," Karis said.

"You can't blame them."

"Because Dad dumped their mother and them, too."

"And never looked back or paid child support or ever sent a single one of them so much as a birthday card."

Karis nodded her understanding. "He wasn't a great dad," she confirmed.

"Not even to you and Lea?"

"Didn't Lea talk to you about him?"

"She didn't talk about any of you. She avoided talking about her family at all except to say that she was the black sheep. At the time we all liked her and assumed that was a good thing."

"So you didn't ask about any of us or about why she was the black sheep?"

"I knew Ted Pratt had deserted one wife and seven kids. I didn't figure that made him much of a father or much of a man. The other Pratts are great people thanks to their mother and the life and upbringing she made sure they had. I thought maybe Lea hadn't had the advantage of a mother like Loretta Pratt to make up for what her father was. So I thought that since she didn't want to get into it, it was all better left alone."

"Well, you were right about Dad not being much of a father. But he was…I don't know exactly what he was—in love with my mother or obsessed with her or something that kept him coming back to her. Lea and I were just sort of footnotes to that."

"Meaning what? That he wasn't living with your mother and playing superdad to you while his first family struggled without him?"

"Is that what people here think? That he left and lived happily ever after with my mom in Denver?"

Luke shrugged, acknowledging the possibility.

"No, that's definitely not how it was. Dad had a home with us, but he didn't spend much time in it. He traveled around selling office equipment and he was gone a lot more than he was home. Plus, while Lea and I were the only other kids he fathered, there was a steady stream of other women he left my mother for. And when he was off with someone else, we didn't see him or hear from him, either—once for nearly two years."

"Seriously?"

"Seriously. But for whatever reason, he always came back to my mom. Sort of like Lea when she would hit bottom and decide she wasn't going to do drugs anymore, Dad would show up full of apologies. He'd beg forgiveness and swear my mother was all he really wanted. He'd say he'd been stupid to ever leave her, that he didn't know what he'd been thinking, that she was the best thing that had ever happened to him. He'd promise he would finally divorce Loretta and marry Mom if only she'd take him back."

"And your mother would?"

"Again and again. There would be fighting and screaming and crying and throwing things. My mother would swear that if he didn't honestly get the divorce and marry her they really were finished. But in the end she just couldn't resist him, I guess, because she'd take him back, he'd never do anything about actually getting a divorce, and everything would be forgotten. Then he'd start all over again, staying away on his business trips for longer and longer, calling home less and less, eventually not calling at all and not coming back. Until the next time he wanted to move in again."

As Karis sat there looking at Luke, at his cologne-ad handsomeness, at those teal green eyes, at that body that wouldn't quit, she had the first inkling of understanding a woman having trouble resisting a man, because Luke was a little irresistible himself.

But she didn't want to think about that, so she continued with what she was saying about her father.

"As for Lea and me, Dad made attempts to play father when he was around, but they were feeble and stilted and he wasn't genuinely interested in having anything to do with us. Occasionally he'd give us some token words of wisdom that were just lame. Or he'd put a half-baked effort into teaching us to ride a bicycle or drive a car—only because Mom had urged him to—and then after about ten minutes he'd lose interest and beg off. Storming Lea's and Abe's trailer that last time was like that. It was something he thought he should step in and do as a father, even though I knew he'd be clumsy at it and not know how to handle it. I tried to convince him not to do it at all, to let me go. But he was trying to make one of his big shows of being a parent and there was nothing I could do to stop him."

"So basically having him around made for a more dysfunctional family than the other Pratts had without him?"

"I never thought of us as *dysfunctional*," Karis said, taking issue. "I'll admit that when it came to our father, Mom had a weak spot and made some choices I didn't agree with—"

"Like getting involved and having two illegitimate kids with a married man with seven other kids and then letting him come back over and over after fooling around with even more women and still not divorcing the one woman he was actually married to?"

"Yes," Karis admitted defensively. "I told you she had a weak spot for him. As his daughter I didn't see the appeal, but women seemed easily charmed by him. My mother most of all. But in every other way she was a good mom. She worked hard to keep a roof over our heads and food in our mouths, to make sure we had everything we needed and wanted. We were loved and cared for and knew we could turn to her for anything. She made sure I had a college education and she stuck with Lea through things a less devoted parent would have washed their hands of. I never thought of us as the kind of family my friends had, but I didn't feel *dysfunctional,* either. I functioned just fine."

She had the sense that he was refraining from reminding her that she'd shown up on his doorstep with everything she owned stuffed in the car she'd intended to sleep in and that didn't speak highly of how well she functioned. But she didn't pursue it.

Instead she glanced at the wallet she was still holding and finally opened it.

It was empty of all but a snapshot of her mother.

"I wondered who that was," Luke said, letting go of their dysfunction debate.

Karis was only too happy to abandon it herself. "This picture is of Mom."

"She's pretty. You look more like her than Lea did."

The compliment lit a tiny warm spot inside Karis that she didn't want to acknowledge. Especially in light of the fact that he considered her dysfunctional.

"What happened to your mother? I assume she's not around, since you're on your own with Amy," Luke said then.

"Mom was killed in a car accident a year and a half ago. I think that's what really prompted Lea to come to Northbridge. We both felt such a loss when Mom was gone. And since we'd always been curious about the *real* Pratts— that's what we called the Pratts here, the *legitimate* Pratts—I think Lea came to try to find people who might fill that gap somehow."

Karis could tell Luke didn't believe that. He still thought Lea had come to Northbridge to do exactly what she'd ended up doing—to steal. Karis knew she couldn't convince him otherwise, so she didn't try.

Besides, it was getting late and seeing Lea's things, seeing their father's wallet, talking about her family, had sapped her. She was tired.

She took the photograph of her mother from its sleeve and closed the wallet.

"I'll keep the snapshot of Mom and give Amy the duck to play with, but the rest of this stuff can either be thrown away or put in a charity box," she said as she replaced it all. "And I don't know about you, but I could use some sleep. It's been a long day."

She saw Luke's nod of agreement out of the corner of her eye, aware that he was watching her very closely again.

"You can leave it all there. We'll deal with it in the morning," he said, pushing himself out of his chair and turning off the lamp on the end table beside the sofa.

Karis was more than willing to leave the box and stood, too, taking with her only the photograph and the duck as Luke motioned with one hand for her to go ahead of him into the entryway and up the stairs.

Oddly, though, once they got to the second floor, Karis discovered she was slightly reluctant to toss him only a simple good-night over her shoulder and continue on to the attic.

Instead she turned to face him in the hallway and said, "I didn't get a chance to tell you before, but I really appreciated your support this afternoon. I know I'm not someone you *want* to support—"

"I just made the introductions and verified your story."

"Still, it was something not to have to face the real Pratts alone and tell them the news."

Luke nodded again, slowly, his eyes staying on her the whole while, the expression on his lean, ruggedly masculine face inscrutable but not forbidding.

"Anyway, thank you," she said.

"You're welcome."

"And I guess I'll see you in the morning."

He nodded once more, but the way he was looking at her made her feel she shouldn't merely turn and leave, as if there was more to come.

And although she had no idea what more there might be, what flashed through *her* head was that he might be considering kissing her.

Which was insane, of course.

She didn't even know why it had crossed her mind. There was no way Luke Walker, of all people, was thinking about kissing her. He didn't even like her. He was holding her car keys hostage because he didn't trust her as far as he could see her. He thought she was trying to pull a fast one on him. Why would he even— or ever—entertain the idea of kissing her?

He wouldn't. It was just her who was thinking about it. Wondering what it might be like. What kind of kisser he might be. How it might feel. Taste. How good it might be to have those big hands of his take her by the shoulders and pull her to him. Those massive arms wrap around her. How good it might be to press her own hands to his chest. To rise up on tiptoe and tilt her head far back so it wouldn't be a simple peck but a genuine, deep, lasting kiss with lips warm and open. With tongues—

Tongues? She was standing there thinking about French-kissing? French-kissing Luke Walker?

Oh boy…

"Well," she said in a hurry, "I'll say goodnight then."

Or had she already said that? She couldn't remember. She couldn't remember anything but that fantasy of having him kiss her. That fantasy that was so, so not what should have ever come into her head, let alone canceled out everything else.

"Yeah," he said after a moment, which made her unwillingly wonder if he could possibly have been lost in similar mental wanderings. "Good night."

Karis nodded as if that was something she needed to agree to and then felt like an idiot, deciding in that instant that she needed to go to her room without any more delay, close the door behind her and get a grip on herself.

But still she said another, unnecessary "See you in the morning" before she turned and made a beeline up the second flight of stairs to the attic bedroom.

Once she got there, she closed the door behind her and stood glued to that spot for a moment, stunned.

Of course there wouldn't be any kissing of Luke Walker, she thought, and there was no reason for it to even flit through her brain.

But now that it had, it was difficult to block out.

In fact, it was nearly impossible, as that fantasy kiss replayed itself yet another time, this one with her eyes shut.

Until she realized that her eyes were indeed closed and she forced them open. Forced herself to stop thinking about kissing and to move away from the door, as if it would put more distance between her and Luke.

Because there was one thing she wasn't, one thing she was determined never to be—a woman with a weak spot for any man.

She'd loved her mother. She'd respected her and admired her in every way except when it came to her father, and then she'd hated that her mother had taken him back again and again. That her mother hadn't been able to resist him, something Karis would never let happen to her.

So she took a deep breath and tried to draw strength from her convictions and from the reminder that Luke was Lea's ex-husband, to shore up that weak spot before any more thoughts of kissing Luke could invade and gain a stronghold.

But it was apparently too late.

Because half an hour later, after she'd slipped into bed and shut her eyes again, there, waiting for her behind her closed lids, was the image of him taking her into his arms and kissing her.

And regardless of how hard she tried, she couldn't get it to go away.

Chapter Five

"So this is Amy now."

It was late Sunday afternoon before Karis, Luke and Amy went to Northbridge's emergency room for the blood draws that would be submitted for DNA testing. Luke had been on duty earlier in the day and, when he'd returned from work, Karis had warned him that they wanted Amy fresh from her nap and well rested in advance of being stuck with a needle, so they'd waited.

The doctor squatting on his haunches, to be at Amy's eye level, was Luke's brother Reid. His response to Karis when Luke introduced them had been professional but a tad chilly—the best she thought she could expect in view of what any of Luke's family or friends must have felt about someone connected to Lea.

He was warmer in his attention to Amy and whether that was how he would have treated any infant or because she was the baby he'd believed to be his niece once upon a time, Karis couldn't tell. She was just grateful he was being kind to her niece.

"Can you say hi?" Karis asked Amy.

Amy was sitting on Karis's lap, warily watching the stranger. Her stuffed elephant was in the crook of one arm so she could put her two middle fingers in her mouth without losing the toy. She made no effort to comply with Karis's request to greet the doctor.

"That's okay. I know you don't remember me," Reid Walker said, nudging Amy's knee before he stood again and spoke to Karis. "I'll need you to hold her tight and steady. With any luck, we can do this fast."

"Okay," Karis said, sorry her niece had to be put through this because of whatever lies Lea had told.

Luke was standing nearby overseeing the proceedings. He'd already had his blood taken in another room and come into this one, along with his brother, when he was finished.

"Can we get our puppeteer in here?" Reid Walker called through the open exam-room door.

A woman Karis assumed to be the nurse joined them, closing the door behind her and kneeling in front of Amy with a snowman finger puppet to distract the child while the doctor pushed up one of Amy's sleeves and tied off her upper arm.

The distraction worked that far. Amy was more interested in the puppet show than in what Reid was doing. Karis hoped the baby might go on watching the nurse and not even notice what was being done to her.

"Hold tight," Reid whispered to Karis just before her hopes were dashed and Amy realized she'd been stuck.

Out came the fingers in her mouth and down fell the elephant to the floor as the baby wailed at the top of her lungs.

"I'm sorry, Amy. We'll be done in just a minute," Reid assured as the nurse gave up the puppet show and rubbed the baby's leg, muttering understanding words to her.

"It's okay, sweetheart. It's okay," Karis said, too, fighting to keep the squirmy baby still for what seemed like the longest blood draw in the history of mankind.

Then it was over and the needle was removed. But Amy continued to cry. Attempts were made to quiet her by showing her a bandage with cartoon characters on it that would be put on the puncture wound, but she didn't care. Instead she seemed to blame Karis for the injury and held out her arms to Luke for rescue.

Surprised, Karis wasn't sure what to do about that. Neither of them had gone within three feet of each other since Karis and Amy had arrived and Luke certainly hadn't made any move to touch the little girl.

But there was Amy, sobbing and beseeching him to take her.

After a moment's hesitation, he stepped up and took her from Karis's lap. And not only did he settle Amy on one hip, he even placed his free hand on her back, held her close and patted her comfortingly.

"She's mad at you," Luke said to Karis over Amy's shoulder, apparently finding that funny, because, for the first time since Karis had met him, he actually smiled.

There was no way it should have thrilled Karis as much as it did. Yes, he had a great smile. It infused his whole face. It made his eyes turn a shade more blue than green. It crinkled tiny lines at their corners. It drew grooves from his nose to his mouth and rounded the planes of his cheeks. It showed straight, perfect white teeth. It smoothed all his rougher edges, brought out a glimmer of devilishness and transformed his handsome face to make him even more appealing.

Seeing it just shouldn't have made her feel as if the sun had finally broken through the clouds.

But it did.

And she didn't develop more immunity to it—or to him—when she watched him cooing to Amy as he swayed a little to soothe her. In fact, Karis was so lost in the sight that for a moment she didn't realize other things were happening around her. The nurse left the room; Reid Walker was talking about getting the samples to the lab ASAP; still Karis was sitting in the chair, the elephant on the floor at her feet, staring at Luke.

When it did register, she retrieved the toy and Amy's coat, and stood to go to Luke and the baby.

Her attempts to make up with her niece failed, though. Amy was having none of that. She buried her face in the side of Luke's neck and wouldn't even look at Karis, which made Luke chuckle—a nice sound to replace Amy's cries now that they had stopped.

"How did I get to be the bad guy here?" Karis complained.

"An Kras ba-guy," Amy repeated, confirming that was what she thought of her aunt.

Luke's winning smile became a grin before he dipped his chin to whisper in the baby's ear, "I think she's sorry. She brought you Eddy."

Amy begrudgingly looked at Karis out of the corner of her baby-blue eyes and stretched out one arm to accept her favorite toy.

Karis handed it over and then rubbed Amy's back as Amy clasped the stuffed elephant to her and continued to seek solace in Luke.

"Will you let me put on your coat?" Karis asked cajolingly.

"No!"

"I'll leave you two to hash this out," Reid said. "Talk to you later, Luke," he added, before exiting the exam room.

In a calming, soft tone of voice, Luke said to Amy, "How about if I put on your coat and we take a little walk? I know where there are puppies you can play with and then maybe we can have some dinner and if you eat it all we can have ice cream after that?"

"'Kay," Amy agreed with a continuing pout, likely not grasping most of what he was suggesting.

Luke took her to the exam table and set her down, accepting her coat from Karis.

Karis stood aside and watched as he put on the baby's heavy winter coat, zipped it and pulled the hood up, too, to tie under Amy's chubby chin. All with big, strong hands and long, thick fingers that were gentle and adept and held Karis's interest more raptly than there was any reason for them to.

She told herself it was purely a matter of gratitude she was feeling. Gratitude for the fact that Luke was putting aside his own resentments, hard feelings and doubts for the sake of the little girl, treating her kindly, caringly, lovingly. That it had nothing whatsoever to do with imagining those same hands on her own skin…

"Is that all right with you?" Luke said.

Karis wasn't sure what he was talking about. She'd obviously missed something while she was enthralled with watching him.

"Is what all right with me?"

"A walk along Main Street, dinner at my brother Ad's restaurant, then ice cream?"

So she'd only missed a few details.

"Sounds great," she said, because it did, especially since the temperature had climbed to a balmy fifty-seven degrees that afternoon.

"It'll mean a colder walk home after dark. Are you up for that?" he asked.

Because of the nice weather, and because his

house was only a block behind Main Street, they'd opted for putting Amy in her stroller and walking to the hospital. Which meant they didn't have a heated car to drive back in. But what he was proposing sounded like such a nice way to finish out the day that Karis was willing to risk it.

"There's an extra baby blanket in the back of the stroller so we can bundle Amy up, and it's a short trip. I'm willing if you are," Karis answered.

"How about you, Amy? Want to see some puppies?"

"Eddy?" Amy said as if puppies and elephants might be the same thing.

"Close," Luke said.

"I see 'em."

"Great. Then that's what we'll do," Luke decreed before casting Karis a glance and adding, "And you can have a little tour of the town."

Karis wasn't sure why this day at the doctor's had taken them another small step away from animosity, but she wasn't going to question it. She was just going to enjoy it. Enjoy being out and about for a while. Enjoy getting to tour the small town she hadn't really had the opportunity to see much of.

Enjoy him…

No, she warned herself against that last part.

She could enjoy the lighter mood, and she could enjoy being out and about, getting to see the town. But that was all.

"Will you come to me now?" she asked her niece, holding out her arms. She was hoping Amy would take her up on the offer so she could have the baby as armor. Armor against whatever it was that was making her aware of the fact that there was more than merely surface allure to Luke Walker when he was being a nice guy.

She was glad that Amy responded by leaning toward her, letting her know that she would allow Karis to hold her again.

"I guess you're forgiven," Luke said.

"Thank goodness for short memories," Karis pronounced, picking up the baby, who handed Luke her elephant, apparently as a consolation.

He chuckled again and accepted it. "Thank you."

They left the five-room hospital and emergency center without fanfare, finding Amy's stroller undisturbed on the sidewalk outside. Karis had been reluctant to leave it there, but Luke had assured her there was no reason to worry.

"See? I told you," he said as Karis put Amy in the stroller and strapped her in. "This is Northbridge—keys can be left in ignitions, doors can be left unlocked, strollers can be left on the sidewalk, and nothing happens."

"So why do they need a police force?" she countered, teasing him even though she was unsure how he would take it.

But he took it well, because it bought her another smile. "Just to keep the mischief and mayhem to a minimum," he said as they headed up Main Street.

Main Street seemed to Karis to be exactly the right name for Northbridge's primary thoroughfare. Quaint, old-fashioned buildings lined the wider-than-average boulevard behind tall, ornate wrought-iron pole lamps circled with flower boxes adorned with autumn decorations. Nuzzled together, the buildings on each block shared side walls with their neighbors and housed shops, stores and businesses that accommodated the foot traffic along the bricked sidewalks.

There were more two- and three-story buildings than single-story structures, many with arches, cornices and gingerbread eaves that added to the nostalgic ambience. Of the two- and three-level establishments, most had overhangs or awnings or patiolike coverings shading their front doors and display windows. Display windows were festooned with pumpkins, gourds, leaves and every variety of Halloween decoration in honor of the holiday that would fall on Tuesday.

Luke gave Karis an abbreviated history as they went past a general store, a Realtor's office, several boutiques and a toy store that also sold nursery furniture and baby clothes. According to the Northbridge native, the town and a fair share of the buildings dated back a hundred years, and some of the businesses continued to be owned and operated by members of founding families.

He seemed to take pride in the history, as well as his own place among the people they encountered, the majority of whom knew him by name and offered pleasantries.

Karis recalled complaints from Lea about just that—everyone knowing everyone else's business, never being able to go out of the house without talking to a dozen people. Karis didn't know if it would wear thin after a while, but at that moment she found it all very appealing. She liked the thought of buildings and businesses enduring through generations, handed down from fathers and mothers to sons and daughters. She liked the sense of stability, of strength that was not only in that endurance but in the way the people seemed to care about one another. She envied ties like that. She envied the sense of community she saw and felt all around her.

When they reached Main Street's end Luke pointed to the other side of the T formed by the cross street and told her that was the Town Square. From the distance Karis could see an octagonal gazebo at the Town Square's heart, also decorated for the upcoming holiday, and it seemed like frosting on the cake of the small town. Even though nothing was going on there right now, she could imagine the gatherings and festivals and holiday celebrations that Luke said were held in the Town Square and how much fun it would be to attend them. And it struck her that, under different circumstances, Northbridge might have been a place where she would have considered starting over. As it was, she couldn't help regretting that wouldn't be an option for her when her ownership of the real Pratts' house became known, along with what she would need to do with it.

Good to his word, Luke took Karis and Amy to see the puppies that were for sale. Their owners had set up a pen in the yard just outside the whitewashed, traditional-looking church with its tall steeple.

There were two litters—four gray terriers

and three hound dogs that appeared to be a big attraction, because Karis, Luke and Amy had to wait their turn to get anywhere near the pen to pet them.

By the time they had, dusk was falling, and after good-naturedly rejecting the puppies' owners' attempts to get him to take one of the dogs, Luke suggested he and Karis take Amy back to Main Street to his brother's restaurant.

Temperatures were falling fast, so Karis agreed it was probably time to cut her tour of Northbridge short, and they headed back up Main Street on the opposite side of the road.

Adz—the restaurant owned by Luke's brother—was across from and slightly north of the medical facility where the afternoon had begun. It looked like an English pub and the place was packed when they got there. But that didn't matter. It was like arriving at a huge family function, and room was made for them near the long bar.

Like their walk, one interruption after another accompanied their meal as other diners stopped by to say hello, to be introduced to Karis, to fuss over Amy and to ask Luke about the ongoing investigation of the old bank robbery and the former Reverend's wife.

Karis didn't mind that she and Luke didn't

have the chance to say more than a few words to each other between interruptions. It all just seemed folksy and friendly to her.

She also didn't mind when, after dinner, Luke was cajoled into a dart game to defend his title as reigning champ.

Even Amy was entertained by the attention she received from everyone who walked by her high chair. And the graham crackers and ice cream their waitress kept her occupied with didn't hurt, either.

It was after nine o'clock before Luke suggested they leave. Amy had had a mellowing cup of warm milk a little while ago and was now half-asleep as Karis bundled her up and put her back in the stroller.

With the extra blanket covering her, she fell fast asleep on the walk back to Luke's house, but both Luke and Karis were feeling the cold when they got there.

"I don't know about you, but I think I need a fire to warm up," Luke said, once he had the front door open and was waiting for Karis to push the stroller and sleeping baby across the threshold. "Want to put Amy to bed and share it?"

"Oh, yeah!" Karis said in the midst of a shiver that shook her as she removed her own coat and then took Amy upstairs to the nursery.

Amy went undisturbed into her pajamas and crib, and Luke was nursing a roaring blaze when Karis joined him in the living room after she'd tucked the baby in for the night.

"Want a glass of wine? Or brandy? Or a cup of hot chocolate?" Luke said when he spotted her return.

"No, thanks. I had enough to eat and drink at your brother's restaurant. I just want some heat!" Karis responded as she sat on the floor in front of the hearth and hugged her knees.

Luke had the single-log fire going strong so he turned to brace his back against the side wall of the fireplace, facing her. He looked at her intently enough to make her uncomfortable, which prompted her to talk.

"But the brother who owns the restaurant isn't the same brother who's the doctor and took blood today at the hospital, right?" she said, building on her previous answer to his question about drinks and trying to get a handle on who was who in his family.

"Reid is who you met today," Luke clarified. "Ad—hence the name of the place as Adz— owns the restaurant."

"Only he wasn't there tonight."

"No. His wife is pregnant and having some major twenty-four-hour-a-day morning sickness, so he's been staying home with her as much as he can."

"Are there just the three of you—you, Ad and Reid? Lea never said."

"There are five of us, plus our mother. Ad, Reid and I also have another brother—Ben— and a sister, Cassie. They're twins. Ben has a placement facility and school just outside of town for boys in trouble, and Cassie was the freshman advisor at the college until she married Joshua Cantrell two weeks ago."

"The tennis-shoe mogul?"

"Yep."

"What about…let's see, who does that leave?" Karis said, figuring out which of his siblings had been matrimonially accounted for and which hadn't. "You said Ad is married and pregnant. Your sister is married to the tennis-shoe guy. I know you're not married. So that leaves Reid and Ben. Are they married?"

"Ben is and his wife is pregnant, too. Further along than Ad's wife, who just found out last week. And Reid's wedding is Wednesday night. They didn't want a big deal so soon after Cassie's wedding, so they decided to just have a low-key family thing right before they leave on their honeymoon."

Karis nodded. "And your mom is still around—"

"Right down the street."

"But your dad? Where is he?"

"He died when I was a little kid."

"I'm sorry."

"Long time ago," Luke said, by way of accepting her condolences but letting her know they were unnecessary after so many years.

"And were you and your brothers and sister all born and raised in Northbridge?"

"Born and raised and still living here with no plans to leave. Well, except Cassie. She spends some of her time in L.A. or New York now with Joshua when he has business to take care of. But they're going to build a house here and the plan is to make Northbridge their home."

"Did you like growing up here?" Karis asked, thinking about how much *she* liked the small town. Or at least what she'd seen of it today.

Luke shrugged a broad shoulder encased in a hunter-green henley shirt that darkened the color of his eyes. "I guess you could say I liked growing up here. I didn't *not* like it and pine for the big city, if that's what you mean. But since I've never grown up anywhere else, I can't tell you if it was better or worse. It was just growing up."

With only one log burning, the fire was

already dwindling. Luke poked at it to keep it going before resettling himself with the side of his right leg on the floor, his left leg raised to brace his arm. Then his gaze went back to Karis.

"What about you?" he asked as if he were genuinely interested. "I know you and Lea and your mother always lived in Denver. Did you wish you were in a small town?"

Karis laughed slightly. "I never thought about it. I guess you're right—you just grow up where you grow up."

"And you grew up without much of a father, huh?" he said, referring to what she'd told him the night before.

"It was pretty much just the three of us— Mom, Lea and me. The three girls."

"You thought of your mother as one of the girls?"

"Well, I did. I suppose that came out of the times Dad would take off. We'd sort of close ranks and hunker down in our disappointment and hurt. And do what we could to boost Mom's spirits, because she'd bottom out and be sad and upset. We'd watch sappy movies and eat chocolate—"

"Ah, that's where the chocolate addiction came from," he said, probably having noted that not only had she been trying to break into her car for the confection the previous evening, but that besides the chocolate ice cream she'd had that afternoon she'd also had a thick, gooey brownie topped with yet another scoop of ice cream and smothered with hot fudge while he'd played darts tonight.

"What about Lea?" he said. "She wasn't into sappy movies or eating chocolate when she was here—for consolation or for any other reason."

"No, she sort of lost interest when she hit her teens. She changed so much then. She only wanted to be with her friends. She started getting into trouble and poor Mom was always having to go to her school or deal with a parent she'd offended or get her out of something. Lea and Mom fought almost all the time."

"But you still went on comforting your mother through her breakups with your father."

"And through the stuff with Lea. I felt even worse for my mother. Not only did she have to deal with my father taking off every time we turned around, but then he'd be gone and she'd have to handle all the Lea stuff, too, without any help or support. It was hard on her and I tried to do what I could to help."

"So you were the responsible one."

"I don't know about that. I know I became the chocolate and sappy-movie provider during the rough patches. And I just tried to stay out of trouble myself, get good grades. Not put any more pressures or demands on my mom. I don't know if that was being responsible or not, I just didn't want to add to the turmoil of my family."

Luke studied her for what seemed like a long while and it warmed her up even more than the fire had.

To such a degree that it made her fidgety and she curved her legs to one side and leaned her weight on one arm just to give herself something to do.

She also searched for more to talk about and settled on returning to the portion of their conversation that was about his childhood in Northbridge.

"So what about the other side of growing up in a small town? You must want to raise your own kids here if you've stayed."

"It's a good place to raise kids. It's safe. It's quiet. Folks look out for each other so you know that even if your kids aren't in your sight, somebody is probably not far away, keeping an eye on them."

"That makes sense. It does seem like one big family here."

"One big, nosy, butting-in family?"

That sounded like a challenge. And like something Lea might have said.

"Because of things like today and tonight with so many people stopping to talk to you?" Karis guessed. "No, I didn't think it was a nosy, butting-in family. I didn't think anybody was being nosy or butting in. I just thought they were being friendly. And I wasn't complaining, if that's what you think. I had a good time today."

He studied her again and Karis was sure he was weighing her words, deciding whether or not she meant them.

Then, as if testing her, he said, "Then maybe you'd like to get into the thick of it again tomorrow. I have an after-work football game—"

"That you're refereeing?"

"No, a bunch of local guys have a team—the Northbridge Bruisers."

"Semi-pros?"

That made him chuckle wryly. "Hardly. We just get together to play whatever's in season to keep in shape. Anyway, tomorrow we have a game. The weather is supposed to be as warm as it was today, so maybe you and Amy can come and watch."

"I'd like that," Karis said, without hesitation and with a grin she couldn't suppress.

"What? Are you laughing at me for some reason?" he demanded when he saw the smile.

"No," she was quick to assure him. "I was

just thinking that between throwing darts and playing football, there really is a side of you that isn't completely stalwart."

"Stalwart?" he repeated, as if it were a dirty word.

"You know, you come off all serious and intimidating. It's kind of funny to find that you really can let your hair down."

She'd apparently embarrassed him, because his answering smile was sheepish and he bowed his head to run his hand over his short hair.

"Not much to let down," he commented, referring to his hair.

He was right. But still the short haircut suited him. Especially since he had a well-shaped head and the lack of locks put more emphasis on his ruggedly great looking face.

Karis wasn't about to say that, though. "I'm just saying that it's nice to see you have some fun in you."

"Oh, I have plenty of fun in me," he countered, looking at her again, his expression and his tone hinting at a touch of wickedness to go with the earlier smile that had shown her there was that to the man, too. There were layers to him that weren't readily apparent—interesting, enticing, sexy layers.

"I should probably get to bed. Amy will have

me up at the crack of dawn," Karis said
suddenly, finding Luke *too* interesting and
enticing and sexy at that moment and knowing
she should nip it in the bud.

Luke glanced over his shoulder at the fire.

"Yeah, I should turn in, too. I didn't figure
we were going to need the fire for long, that's
why I made it small," he added, using the poker
to break up the log so there were merely embers
that were safer to leave unattended.

Then he put the poker in the bucket of fireplace tools and got to his feet, offering Karis a
hand to help her up.

His gesture took her by surprise and, because
she didn't want to reject the courtesy and dis-
courage the much, much more amiable tone
that had been achieved between them, she
accepted his help.

And just that quick that hand she had
imagined on her instead of on Amy that afternoon actually did encase her own hand. Tiny
lightning bolts seemed to shoot up her arm,
and she suffered the terrible urge to have her
hand stay in his, to go on feeling the strength,
the power, the warmth of it sluicing all
through her.

But then she was on her feet, too, and he let

go. And her hand closed into a fist as if that could keep the sensation.

Luke didn't seem to notice as he turned off the lamp and they went together up the stairs.

On the second floor Karis peeked into the nursery, making sure Amy was still sleeping before closing the door all but a crack and turning to say good-night to Luke.

Before she could speak, he gave her a lopsided smile and said, "So, you aren't bearing any grudge because she blamed you for the blood test today and came to me?"

"Yeah, what was that, anyway?" Karis said, pretending to be miffed by her niece's desertion. "Little traitor."

"Hey, you were the one holding her down to have needles stuck in her—who turned on who?"

"And you just ate it up," Karis teasingly accused.

"Yes, I did," Luke confessed, grinning the grin that was deadly to her resistance.

"Creep."

"Uh-uh, no name-calling," he chastised.

But it was all in good fun. Good fun that somehow had them ending up standing there in the midst of the bedroom doors on the second floor, facing each other without much space separating them.

Facing each other with eyes meeting in playful standoff.

Eyes meeting and holding.

Lingering, actually.

And his were beautiful eyes, Karis couldn't help thinking. Deep and soulful and alight with mischief all at once. Delving into hers, as if they could see into the center of her. Maybe liking what he saw the way she couldn't help liking what she saw...

Then he leaned forward just slightly, but enough so that she noticed it. Enough so that it was undeniable. So that she honestly thought he was going to kiss her.

But he didn't come close enough to do that. And it flashed through her mind that she needed to go the rest of the way. That he was waiting to see if she wanted him to kiss her.

And she did.

She wished she didn't.

But she did.

And before she could stop herself, she was leaning toward him, too. She was tilting her chin. Raising up on tiptoe.

Kissing him...

She was kissing *him!*

Oh, no! How had *that* happened?

She honestly didn't know. She just knew it

shouldn't have. That *she* shouldn't have kissed *him.* That if there was going to be kissing, it should have been *him* kissing *her.*

So she stopped.

She pulled back, stepped away from him, kept her gaze on his broad chest rather than look him in the eye again and, in a panic, said, "I don't know why I did that! That was dumb! That was bad—"

"It's okay," he said softly, his voice lower than usual.

"It's not okay. I'm sorry—"

"It's what I was going to do before the *stalwart* part of me took control."

He was making a joke. He was letting her off easy. But was he telling the truth?

Karis ventured a glance at his face and couldn't tell.

"Really. It's okay," he said, amused.

Karis shook her head, too embarrassed to say more and turned to flee up the attic steps to her room in mortification.

She closed the door tightly behind her and leaned her forehead hard against it. With her eyes pinched shut, she listened to the sound of Luke not going into his own room the way she'd expected, but retreating all the way down the stairs to the ground floor.

Maybe he was afraid to go to bed himself, she thought. Afraid she'd follow him, corner him, jump him or something.

Then she heard him return to the level just below her.

She heard him climb the attic steps.

She heard him knock on her door....

"Go away," she whispered, too softly for him to hear.

But afraid that he wouldn't do that and wondering what was going to happen next, she opened her eyes without raising her head.

Which left her looking down at the floor just in time to see one of her bite-size chocolate bars slip under the panel.

Karis had to laugh. She just couldn't help it.

"Thanks," she said, this time loudly enough for her voice to carry out to him.

"Anytime," he called back, finally on his way to his own room.

Chapter Six

"Afternoon, boys."

It *was* afternoon—Monday afternoon—when Luke and Cam Pratt arrived at the home of Reverend Armand Perry.

The seventy-eight-year-old man, who had seen to most of Northbridge's spiritual needs from the moment he'd taken the pulpit at twenty-nine until retiring four years ago, looked rested and relaxed and not at all concerned by the fact that two of the local police officers had come to question him.

"Reverend," Luke responded to the greeting. "Thanks for seeing us."

The Reverend, who was average height and slight of build, was not seeing Luke and Cam alone, however. His two sons, Carl and Jack, had come in from Billings where they ran a freight business. Three of the seven Perry grandchildren were also there lending moral support—Eve and Faith, who were two of Jack's three daughters, and one of Carl's four offspring, his son Jared.

Because Luke and Cam had grown up with the Perry grandchildren and were within the same age range, they all knew each other. Luke and Cam were offered seats on dining-room chairs that had apparently been brought into the formal living room for the occasion, and more greetings were exchanged before Luke got down to business.

"You all know what's going on with the investigation of the bank robbery and Celeste," he began.

"It's in the newspapers every day," the Reverend said. "Has something new brought you here today?"

"As a matter of fact, it has," Cam answered. "There's a woman in Bozeman who read about this in the newspaper last week and called the Bozeman police. She said she worked with a woman in 1962 who she'd become friends with and who might have been Celeste. The woman—she'd called herself Charlotte Pierce—had claimed to have family—sons—in Northbridge. She wanted to do whatever she could to see them again."

"The name Charlotte Pierce isn't familiar to me, if that's what you want to know," the Reverend offered.

"The name was an alias," Luke said. "And those few months in Bozeman are where the trail for that particular Charlotte Pierce begins and ends. So it seems possible—in fact we're thinking it was likely—that it was Celeste."

"And since we have a good indication that she actually did get as close as Bozeman, it doesn't seem a stretch to think she might have snuck back into town at some point," Luke said.

"I told you, I don't know any Charlotte Pierce," Reverend Perry insisted.

"Still, it's a good bet the woman *was* your wife, sir," Luke said, "which puts her less than a day's drive from here."

"And what we're asking," Cam added, "is if any of you had contact with someone who *might* have been Celeste."

"Or if, Reverend," Luke added, "she ever wrote you or called you, trying to smooth the waters, maybe. Or just attempting to see Jack or Carl again. And if, say, you let her know that wasn't going to happen and she gave you an idea of where you could reach her if you ever changed your mind."

"Do you believe that if I had information like that I wouldn't have gone to the authorities with it at the time?"

"No offense, Reverend, but she *was* your wife and the mother of your children," Luke said.

"True," the elderly man confirmed, without expanding on it or addressing any of the questions that had been posed.

Cam tried again. "So was there ever any kind of contact—either from Celeste or from someone who might have been Celeste in disguise using a different name?"

Reverend Perry shook his head. "Sorry, boys, but I don't know what to tell you. Nothing like that happened."

"After she left the night of the robbery, you never heard from her again?" Cam asked.

"I think she would have known there was no going back after what she did."

Luke looked to the Reverend's middle-aged sons. "What about you, Carl, Jack? Did either of you ever hear from her or have any contact with her again? Or with a woman who might have been her?"

Both men shook their heads.

"None I recall," Carl answered.

"Me neither," Jack said.

"It could have even been years later," Cam countered, in an attempt not to have them so easily discard the idea. "And she could have looked completely different. Think about whether you ever encountered a woman who showed an unusual interest in you. Someone you didn't know from around here—you know that isn't something that happens often."

Again both men responded in the negative.

"Eve? Faith? Jared? She could have approached any of the grandchildren, too," Luke said.

They all assured him they hadn't had any contact with anyone who stuck out in their minds, nor had they ever heard of any of their siblings having one.

"We wouldn't have recognized her even if she had come up to us on the street, though," Faith contributed. "The photograph of her in the paper is the first time I've ever seen her."

The rest of the grandchildren concurred.

"We know that Celeste had begun to put on weight within two months of leaving North-bridge," Luke said in order to pursue what was coming to seem more and more like a dead end.

"That Dorian, the bank robber, left her because she was *letting herself go*—that's one of the things he told the FBI. We don't have any idea how much weight she might have gained or how else she might have changed her appearance, but it could have been substantial. A woman, in particular, can alter her looks considerably just with hair and makeup."

"Celeste wasn't allowed to wear makeup," the Reverend insisted.

"But that's the point. She may have started to wear it and been able to alter her look drastically," Cam suggested.

"The weight gain itself could be important here," Luke said. "It might help to know if there was a family history of obesity, if maybe her mother or grandmother or a sister was heavy and *how* heavy. And if you had a picture of them, that would possibly give us an indication of what Celeste could have looked like—or still could look like—at a larger size. Seeing something like *that* might spark a memory."

"There were several members of her family that were very large—obese, in fact—but I don't have photographs of any of them. And they've all passed away now," Reverend Perry answered definitely. Curtly, even.

"Dad didn't keep pictures of Mother or of

any of her family," Jack added. "That's why the only photograph circulating now is that old one from the newspaper article introducing them to Northbridge when we first got here."

"Destroying every image of her or of her family was a rash act by a scorned man," the Reverend said unapologetically. "Something I'm sure you understand, Luke."

Luke didn't address the comment. And it was obvious the elderly man's attitude toward this line of questioning was changing, because, as he continued, he sat up straighter in his wing chair. He sounded much less patient and more as if he were taking Luke and Cam to task.

"I have to say that this whole thing seems like a waste of your time and the taxpayer's money. My understanding is that no one ever thought Celeste had anything to do with the bank robbery. And if the second robber was killed, he undoubtedly wasn't killed by Celeste. He had to have been killed by his partner, who is now deceased himself. So if Celeste committed no crime and wouldn't need to be a witness to convict anyone who did, what's the point in digging all this up again now?"

"It's an open case, Reverend, that could now have a murder attached to it," Cam said. "A crime Celeste *may* have played a part in."

"And while we know you," Luke added, "and don't want to put you or your family through this, we don't have a choice. Evidence of even an old crime—particularly a murder, which carries with it no statute of limitations—needs to be investigated. If Cam and I weren't sitting here with you right now, state authorities would be."

"Are you saying that if Celeste was located, she could be arrested and tried for murder?" the Reverend asked as if the thought was outlandish.

"We won't lie to you," Cam said. "There's that chance."

"Well then, I have to tell you, I hope you *don't* find her," Reverend Perry said. "Because while I certainly bear Celeste no warm feelings, I don't believe she was capable of committing either a bank robbery or a murder, and to drag her—if she's even still living—and the rest of us through what a trial would entail for no good reason would be a travesty."

The elderly man's voice was loud and his face had turned red by the time he'd finished speaking. Carl, who was standing behind his father's chair, placed a hand on the Reverend's shoulder. "They're only doing their job, Dad."

"I think that's about all he can take for today, though, guys. Can we end this now?" Jared Perry asked.

Jared, Luke and Cam were all friends, so the request wasn't hostile.

After exchanging a look that said they knew they weren't getting anywhere, Luke and Cam conceded.

They both stood.

"I'm sure it goes without saying," Luke said, "but if any of you think of anything or remember anything—regardless of how inconsequential it might seem—please give us a call."

Agreements were muttered by everyone except the Reverend.

"We'll find our own way out," Cam assured them before he and Luke said goodbye and left.

The Reverend's house was a block behind the church and only a short distance from the police station, so Luke and Cam had walked over. Neither of them spoke until they were several yards away from the house and then Luke said, "I wondered if we would hit a nerve today."

"You think the Reverend is ticked off that this whole thing is coming back to haunt him or does he know more than he's saying?"

"Speaking from experience," Luke responded, "the past rearing its ugly head again when you least expect it is not something anybody can be too happy about. But that doesn't mean I'm convinced he doesn't know more than he's saying."

"What if it were you?" Cam asked, treading lightly.

"You mean would I protect Lea forty years from now?"

"Or would you withhold information to protect yourself from having what you went through with her brought up and rehashed and talked about all over again?"

Luke gave a wry, humorless chuckle. "Probably for my own sake I'd be tempted to keep quiet. Especially if any contact she'd made had come and gone decades ago."

"What if that wasn't the case? What if even forty-plus years later, you knew where she was?"

Luke glanced at Cam. "You think he knows where she is?"

Cam shrugged. "He was damn touchy during our conversation."

"He was—you're right. But there hasn't been any other sign of her—or of Charlotte Pierce— in Bozeman since that waitress said Charlotte Pierce quit the diner."

"It'd be funny if it *was* Celeste and she quit the diner, gave herself *another* name, and came back here without ever being recognized, wouldn't it? If she's right under our noses some-where?" Cam proposed with a wry laugh.

"And has been since the sixties? I don't know

if it would be funny, but it'd be *something*," Luke said just as they were waylaid by Northbridge's oldest citizen.

Ninety-seven-year-old Miss Georgia Simpson was taking her daily constitutional and stopped to chat with everyone she encountered.

After listening to an account of the ancient woman's ailments, Miss Georgia moved on and so did Luke and Cam. But neither of them continued postulating about Celeste Perry. Instead, Cam ventured back into touchy territory with Luke.

"So along the lines of the past rearing its ugly head again for you…"

"Uh-huh," Luke said.

He'd known Cam was going to want to talk about Karis and Amy. This was the first time Luke had seen any of the other Pratts alone. And of course they had to be curious.

"What's your take on Karis?" Cam asked.

"You're asking me? The brain trust who married her sister after four days?"

Cam laughed. "You've had about that long with this sister and haven't married her yet, I'm figuring you've learned your lesson."

Luke wasn't sure he had. Not with the way things were going with Karis. Not when he'd been on the verge of kissing her the night before. Not when even though he'd managed to talk himself out of kissing her, he'd still liked that *she'd* kissed *him*.

But there was no way he was telling Cam *that*.

"The verdict's still out on this sister," he said.

"But you let her into your house anyway?"

"See? You're thinking my judgment isn't all that great."

"No, I'm thinking there have to be extenuating circumstances. I'm just not sure what they are," Cam allowed.

"The only extenuating circumstance is the possibility that I'm Amy's father."

"Ah," Cam said, as if that explained it. "And you might be Amy's father again according to…"

"According to what Karis says Lea told her."

"So Karis didn't only come here to tell us about the deaths in the explosion," Cam said, making it clear he'd believed all along that there was more going on than had been presented to him and his family on Saturday.

"No, she didn't only come about the deaths," Luke confirmed. "She also came to bring me Amy. She says, because of things that led up to the explosion, she can't keep the baby."

"What things?"

"I haven't been privy to that information. All I know is that she showed up at my door wanting to hand over Amy because Lea told her there *is* the chance Amy's mine even though she claimed otherwise when she took off."

"And for what reason did she say you weren't, if you might be?"

"She wanted a clean getaway—that's the story. And since Karis says she now only has twelve dollars to her name and everything else she owns is in her car, she needed me to step up when it came to Amy."

"So you took them both in?"

"I think there's a better-than-even chance that Amy isn't mine, but until the DNA test I'm having done tells me for sure, what was I going to do? If she *is* mine, I have a responsibility to her. If she isn't, there was no way I was going to let Karis leave her with me and then drive off, probably never to be seen again. So yeah, I guess you could say I took them both in. I also took Karis's car keys so she couldn't disappear and stick—" Luke stumbled over the word that had riled Karis the night she'd shown up on his doorstep. He amended it to, "I took her car keys to keep her here, so I could make sure I didn't end up raising a kid who isn't mine."

"That makes sense. But it still doesn't answer my original question."

"What's my take on Karis?" Luke reiterated. "I'm not sure."

"In other words, we'd all better look out."

Luke didn't know why, but he felt a little guilty giving Cam that impression. "I don't know," he said honestly. "She's Lea's sister—that raises a big red flag all on its own. She showed up here out of the blue the same way. But…" Luke shrugged. "She's better with Amy than Lea was during those five weeks—"

"When you had to do everything for Amy when you weren't at work, and your mother had to do everything when you were, because Lea was too tired and listless to do anything but go out for lunch and shop for new clothes and have her hair done and—"

"There wasn't much maternal instinct to Lea, that's for sure. I was surprised she even took Amy with her when she left. I figured it was because Amy really wasn't mine. But with Karis," he said, "you'd think Amy belonged to her. Unless she's an award-winning actress, the thought of leaving Amy with me when she got here was killing her. And she takes good care of her. I don't think she even likes it if Amy shows an interest in me. Plus…"

Luke paused, really analyzing for the first time what he'd seen so far in Karis. But even as he did, he still wasn't confident in his opinions. Not when, despite the fact that he was fighting it, he seemed to be growing more attracted to her with each passing day.

"I don't know," he repeated.

"Your gut isn't telling you anything?"

It had been telling him to kiss her last night. How could he trust that?

"My gut told me to marry Lea," he reminded.

"What does that mean? That your gut is telling you to marry this one, too?"

"No! Jeez, I'm not crazy. Or at least being crazy once was my limit. I'm just saying that even if my gut is telling me Karis might not be like Lea, that she might be a responsible, honest, upstanding person, a person who may have been as victimized by Lea as we were—"

"You think Lea swindled her? Or robbed her?"

"Like I said, I haven't been privy to that information. But even if my gut is allowing for the possibility that Karis might be on the up-and-up, I'm still reserving judgment. And being careful."

"So you're not condemning her just because she's Lea's sister, but you don't trust that she's what she appears to be, either?"

"I started out condemning her because she's Lea's sister," Luke admitted. "But let's just say that so far I haven't had reason to hang on to that."

"But you're also being cautious about buying what she's selling," Cam persisted.

Luke knew he wasn't being as cautious as he should be when kissing had entered the picture. When he'd left her the night before wishing he'd had more of a chance to experience the kiss that had been there and gone before he knew it. More of a chance to enjoy it. To prolong it.

To do it again…

"I'm trying to be cautious, yeah," he said. "But just between you and me? There's some charm to Karis."

"Lea's kind of charm? She didn't strike me that way."

"No, Karis's personality is completely different from Lea's. She's not the party girl Lea was."

"That seems like a plus."

"A big plus."

"So what *is* her charm?"

Luke felt as if he were stepping onto thin ice even thinking about it. To describe what he kept attempting to ignore.

Attempting unsuccessfully to ignore.

But still he said, "Karis doesn't seem to need to be the center of attention the way Lea did. She doesn't do that coy little-girl act to get her way. Karis's charm is sort of quiet. It sneaks up on you. She can make me laugh, sometimes out of nowhere. She can take teasing and dish it out herself. She's agreeable but not a pushover. She's proud. Independent. I haven't gotten the impression that she's come in with her hand out. I think she would have starved rather than let me feed her, until I made a deal with her to exchange housecleaning services for room and board. And she's making good on the deal, because I left her at home doing just that."

"That's definitely not Lea. She had us all buying her lunch and dinner and drinks, not to mention that she went behind Mara's and Neily's backs and put clothes on their tabs at the stores around town."

"No, I don't think that's Karis. But who knows for sure at this point?"

"So you think we should all be careful but maybe not punish her for her sister's crimes," Cam summarized.

"Yeah, I guess maybe I'd say that."

"And she *is* our half sister," Cam conceded somewhat reluctantly.

"And no matter who Amy's father is, Amy is your niece," Luke pointed out.

"Yeah, I kind of tend to lose sight of that."

"But I still wouldn't say to jump in with both feet. Just maybe cut Karis a little slack, and wait and see."

"That seems fair," Cam said as they reached the station house.

That ended the conversation, but still Luke went back to work thinking that the advice he'd just given his friend was good advice to take himself—wait and see.

Wait and see what Karis was really all about.

Wait and see if she showed any signs that she might not be any better than her sister.

Just wait—that was the operative word.

Definitely wait when it came to kissing or to anything else that didn't keep him at a safe distance from those quiet charms and the attributes he'd just outlined for Cam.

Because Karis's effect on him was still potent even if she wasn't as out there as her sister had been. In fact, her effect was almost more potent because she *wasn't* as out there. Because her charm and attributes weren't all on the surface. Because there was some substance to them. Because Karis herself seemed to have more substance than Lea had ever demonstrated.

And it honestly was all just sneaking up on him, the way he'd told Cam. Getting under his skin. Even when he was trying not to let it happen.

Which meant that his only hope was whatever distance he could achieve in order to maintain some objectivity.

Objectivity and indifference and disinterest and detachment—that was what he needed and he knew it. As a cop, he knew it.

And then he passed the candy machine.

And just the thought of Karis's affinity for chocolate, the memory of her laughter through the door the night before when he'd slipped the candy bar under it, her *"Thanks,"* made him smile.

And that was when he added something else to the list of what he knew.

He knew he was kidding himself.

That complete objectivity, indifference, disinterest and detachment were already out of his reach.

Because he liked her.

He didn't want to, but he did.

Which was why he couldn't trust his opinions of or his gut feelings about her.

But it was also why it was all the more important to wait and see.

To wait and see how her being there, the DNA test—everything—played out.

It was tough, though. And it wasn't made any less difficult because he was having so much trouble not thinking about her. Not wanting to be with her every time he wasn't. Not drifting into fantasies about her when he was lying in bed at night staring at the ceiling and picturing her in the attic right above him.

But he had to do it, he told himself firmly. He had to put all he had into resisting every draw, every pull, every appeal.

He had to.

He'd just been duped too badly before to take any chances.

He *wouldn't* take any chances that it might happen again.

So no matter how much he might like Karis, no matter how much he might have wanted to kiss her the night before, no matter how much he'd been wondering ever since she'd kissed him what it might have been like if they'd made a better stab at it, no matter how much he wanted a second try, he wouldn't do it. He couldn't do it.

But damn, did he want to.

Chapter Seven

"How do you think I should play this?" Karis asked Amy as she changed the baby's diaper at three-thirty Monday afternoon.

"Pay?" Amy parroted with her version of *play*.

The fifteen-month-old grabbed the hem of her white turtleneck T-shirt with the pink rosebuds on it and pulled it up in front of her face. A moment later she yanked it down and said, "Pee-boo-see-you."

Amy loved peekaboo and apparently that was what she'd chosen to play.

It wasn't what was on Karis's mind, however. What was on Karis's mind was what had been on Karis's mind since it had happened the night before—the fact that she'd kissed Luke.

"Yes, peekaboo," she answered Amy before getting back to what she'd been talking about in the first place. "Should I just be cool? Should I act like nothing ever happened? Or like I go around kissing men all the time so it was nothing to me?"

"Coo," Amy responded.

"Cool, huh? I don't know. Maybe I should apologize. Or maybe I should say I don't know what made me do it."

Amy did peekaboo again, clearly not as overwrought by Karis's predicament as Karis was.

"I thought I'd hit it lucky this morning because he had already left for work when we went downstairs. But what if he was dodging me? What if he ducked out of the house so he didn't have to see me until he'd decided what to say to me? What if he comes back and says something embarrassing? Not that he could say *anything* about it that wouldn't make it all the more embarrassing. I shouldn't have ever done it, you know? It was just so dumb!"

"Dumb."

"And I've been thinking about it and thinking about it—I haven't been able to think about anything else—and I thought by now I would have come up with what to do or how to act or what to say. But no, I spent the whole day thinking that if I was going to do something this stupid I should have done it better than I did. I should have done it at least long enough so I'd know what it was like, instead of having all this humiliation and still wondering what it really might be like to kiss him."

"Kiss?" Amy said, puckering up.

That got a little laugh out of Karis, who dipped down and kissed her niece the way they did when they were saying good-night or goodbye.

"Thank you," Karis said afterward. "But that doesn't solve my problem."

"Prah-um," Amy echoed as Karis readjusted the baby's T-shirt to tuck into her corduroy pants.

"Yes, problem. Big, huge problem that I don't know what to do about. Maybe we shouldn't go to this game today. Maybe I could leave him a note downstairs and we could hide out up here until he's gone. Maybe I'll think of what I should do by the time he comes back later."

"Go bye-bye," Amy demanded.

Karis couldn't help laughing again. "So you are listening. And you remember me telling you we were going bye-bye this afternoon."

"Go bye-bye," the baby repeated insistently.

"You don't understand—I *kissed* him. Your

mom's ex-husband. Who already thinks I'm some awful, horrible person—"

"I don't think you're an awful, horrible person."

Karis jumped in startled fright at the sound of Luke's deep voice coming from the doorway behind her. She didn't turn to face him or so much as glance over her shoulder at him. Instead, she closed her eyes and grimaced.

"Fuh-ee face," Amy said, squealing on her.

When Karis opened her eyes, Luke was standing at the head of the changing table, having gotten there soundlessly and startling Karis all over again.

"That is a pretty funny face," he agreed with the baby.

The small, crooked smile on his own magnificent mug showed amusement that didn't help Karis's embarrassment one iota.

"Hi!" Amy greeted him then, looking backward up at him.

"Hi, Amy," he answered.

"How long were you there?" Karis asked, mentally going through all she'd just said to her niece and hoping he hadn't heard any but the last of it.

"Long enough."

"How long?" she persisted.

"Uh, I believe it was about the time you were

telling Amy that you should have done it better than you did."

Oh, he'd been standing there way, way too long. Karis could feel her face suffusing with color.

"I can go for the candy bars if you need one," he offered jokingly, obviously because he could see her blush and probably signs of the panic she was feeling, too.

"No," she said. "But it's rude not to let a person know you're there and listen to what she's saying," she chastised.

"It's okay."

"It's not okay. Eavesdropping is not okay."

"I was talking about the kiss last night," he qualified. "It's no big deal."

"It's a huge deal," she muttered to herself, as she sat Amy up on the table and began to brush the baby's curls.

"We can just forget it," Luke said.

Maybe he could. But Karis knew better than to think she could. Especially when she'd been scouring her memory ever since to recall any detail of that kiss, anything about what it had felt like, tasted like, if it might have been any good at all.

"I don't think I can just forget it," she said, although in a tone that revealed her discomposure but not the curiosity and titillation that was keeping it company. "I'm sorry," she said, deciding on the spot that was the tack to take. "I shouldn't have done it."

"And now you can't just let go of it?" Luke asked, shifting his weight onto one uniform-clad hip that told Karis he'd arrived home from work and immediately come looking for her.

"That's easy for you to say, but no, I can't just let go of it. Not when I was the one who—"

Karis didn't see it coming. But all of a sudden Luke raised a hand to lay along her cheek and leaned across the corner of the changing table to kiss her.

Only his wasn't the hit-and-run job that hers had been. There he was, gently guiding her face upward with his big hand. His warm breath was against her skin. His mouth was only softly on hers. His lips were parted and smooth and supple and agile, not too wet and not too dry, sweet and sensual and so, so sexy, moving in a circular motion that took her from shock to reverie to closing her eyes once more and kissing him back.

The kiss deepened, intensified, and set everything inside of her atingle as his hand slid around and into her hair, bringing her closer. Lips parted further and Karis raised her hand to his forearm to aid the cause....

But just about that time the circles slowed and she knew he was drawing the kiss to a close without any idea how much she didn't want him to.

And she *didn't* want him to!

But she took her hand from his arm to keep him from knowing that just as the circles stopped and his hand left her face.

And then it was over.

And she wished it wasn't.

She opened her eyes. She knew she must look as dazed as she felt, but she couldn't help it.

"Now we're even and you can relax," Luke said, his voice more gravelly than it had been before, making a lie of the apathy his tone tried for.

Karis thought they were far from being even. He'd kissed her much more soundly, much more thoroughly than she'd even thought about kissing him, but still she said, "Even," repeating it the same way Amy bounced her own words back to her.

"And since there's no more guessing or wondering on either of our parts what it would have been like, we can stop thinking about it and pretend it never happened."

So he'd been thinking about it and wondering the same as she had.

"And we won't ever do it again," he added.

Something sank inside Karis at that declaration. But she knew he was absolutely right.

"No, never again," she agreed, wanting badly to do it again then and there.

"It's out of our systems and we can put it behind us," he said.

Mission accomplished.

Except that Karis didn't feel as if anything was out of her system, and she had the sense that it wasn't really out of his, either.

But once again she agreed. "It's history."

"History," he confirmed.

Except those beautiful green eyes of his went on looking into hers, intangibly connecting them, holding them in the moment and the one before it when his mouth had been over hers. And to Karis it was almost as if they were reliving the kiss that was still so vivid in her mind.

Until Amy said, "Wha's at?" and wiggled around on the changing table to grab Luke's badge.

Luke blinked as if he'd just been called out of a trance, glancing down at Amy then.

"Pitty," the baby said, decreeing the badge pretty, as if it were a piece of jewelry.

"Are you ready to go bye-bye?" Luke asked her, obviously having heard that portion of

Amy's and Karis's exchange, too, and now using it to alter the focus.

"Bye-bye!" Amy said excitedly, looking next at Karis to repeat it, as if Luke had overruled Karis's earlier mention of possibly not going.

"I just need to change and we can leave," Luke told Karis, business as usual.

"I'll get Amy bundled up and meet you downstairs," she said, hating that her own voice was still weak, but it was the best she could do.

"Bring a lot of blankets. It's nice out now, but it'll be cold before we're through," Luke advised, moving away from the changing table and heading for the door.

As he walked out of the room without a backward glance, Karis couldn't help wondering if he honestly would be able to go on as if nothing had happened between them. And never do it again.

Because as much as she wished for the strength and stamina to genuinely, firmly and forever put both kisses behind her, as much as she told herself she had to abide by the never-again rule, she didn't have a whole lot of confidence in herself.

Not after *that* kiss.

By eight o'clock that night Karis couldn't quite believe what this day had wrought, where she was at that moment, and what was going on around her.

The afternoon's kiss had rocked her, but she'd decided to work at adopting Luke's over-and-done-with attitude. On the surface at least. So she'd gone to his football game putting great effort into not thinking about the kiss and trying not to ogle him on the football field.

That cause had been aided when her half sisters Neily and Mara had joined her on the blanket she'd spread out for her and Amy to sit on.

Neily and Mara hadn't made the overtures early in the game, so Karis was reasonably sure it had taken some discussion on their part. But she had the impression that in the end, Amy had been the draw, because the baby was who they were the most warm and friendly to at first.

By the time the football game had come to its conclusion though, they'd been less guarded with Karis, too, and had invited her, Luke and Amy to their house for pizza.

Pizza and beer had become lively conversation with Amy being passed around and played with and treated like the adorable baby she was.

And even Karis, as she sat in the living room with all seven of her half siblings, felt as if she'd reached a tentative level of acceptance that was almost as good as the kiss that had begun the changes in this day.

It was just so nice to be a part of a group. To be included, to be asked her opinions, even to be teased a little the way the rest of the Pratts freely teased and taunted each other and Luke. And it gave her the chance to watch and begin to get to know these people she was related to.

To know that not only did they all resemble one another enough to be recognized as relatives, but to see that there were things in each of them that reminded her of herself or of Lea or of Amy. To discover that Cam, the cop, had a more mellow side to him even if he was still keeping his distance from her. That Neily and Mara joined forces against their brothers to form the united front of sisters when the brothers were trying to pull rank on them and make them wait on them. That the triplets— Boone, Taylor and Jon—were difficult to tell apart but not impossible. That Cam and Scott seemed to be best friends and looked so much like each other and like the man who had fathered them all that they could have been twins themselves. And that the seven North-bridge Pratts shared a closeness that Karis couldn't help envying.

When dinner was finished, she asked if she

could see the rest of the house and, feeling an even greater sense of guilt for using the occasion to her advantage, she got to see the entire place.

It really was a beautiful old house that was probably worth more than she'd thought before. Which was good. Hopefully that would make at least one portion of her plan easier.

But still she couldn't bring herself to say anything to her half siblings. Especially not when she knew it would ruin the evening she was enjoying so much.

After showing her around, everyone regrouped in the living room for dessert, and the conversation turned to the hottest topic of the day.

"Didn't you and Cam talk to the Reverend today?" Mara asked Luke then.

"We did," Luke confirmed.

"We didn't learn much, though," Cam contributed. "Except that talking about Celeste riled him up."

Cam went on to outline the meeting with the elderly man.

When he'd finished, Luke said, "Cam thinks Reverend Perry might not have been too honest with us. That Celeste *did* contact him at some point and he's just not admitting it. Cam thinks Celeste might even be right under our noses now."

"I didn't say I *thought* that," Cam amended. "I just said wouldn't it be funny if she was."

"It does seem logical that if Celeste was obsessed with seeing her kids again and got as close as Bozeman, she wouldn't stop there," Scott said, supporting Cam.

"And what if she kind of tiptoed into town one day and discovered that no one recognized her?" Mara postulated. "If I were her, I might have stayed."

"Is there any evidence that the Reverend's wife ever came into Northbridge?" Boone asked reasonably.

"No, there's no evidence," Cam admitted. "But Bozeman isn't that far away."

"Is it really possible for anyone to look so different they could come *here* without being recognized?" Jon said as if he didn't think so.

Neily handed Amy to Taylor, who was enticing the baby with an offer to share his dessert, and then said, "Jon has a point. I was at the grocery store yesterday and Lotty Haskell spotted a new mole on the back of Mr. Drake's neck waiting in line. If not even *that* went without notice, how could a whole person come in and not be recognized."

"The Reverend did admit that there was obesity in Celeste's family and we know she was gaining weight almost from the day she left. She could have packed on a lot in two or three years' time," Luke conceded.

Karis was unduly thrilled to feel free to put in her own two cents' worth and did. "Weight can make a real difference," she said. "I had a friend all the way through school who was always the *big girl,* and because she hated the way she looked, she never paid any attention to her hair, never wore makeup, couldn't have cared less about her clothes. Then she went away to college, did some kind of diet-and-exercise program and lost a hundred and fifty-seven pounds. That made her want to do the whole makeover thing—hair, makeup, wardrobe—and when she came home for the first time after it was all done, *I* didn't even recognize her. She looked like a completely different person. So I know for a fact that it's possible."

"But from what's getting talked about," Mara countered, "I've had the impression that Celeste was *very* appearance-conscious. That was part of the conflict with the Reverend—she didn't like being his church-mouse wife. She wanted to dress up, and she always had her hair done at the beauty shop—"

"He made it clear today that he didn't let her wear makeup," Luke said.

"Maybe," Mara continued, "but I also heard that she scandalized the Reverend a few times when they first moved here by wearing short-shorts and a midriff top. It doesn't seem as if someone who cared about how she looked, who probably *would* have worn makeup if her oppressive husband had let her, someone who—I heard, too—jazzed herself up quite a bit when the fling with the bank robber was in full swing before they left town…it just doesn't seem as if someone like that would go to the other extreme and let herself be unrecognizably heavy and unkempt."

"It doesn't seem likely to me, either," Neily said.

"But if she wanted to be near her kids badly enough and the weight was packing on anyway…" Taylor countered.

"How bad could she have wanted to be with her kids if she left them in the first place?" Boone argued.

"But if she did come back into town a gazillion years ago looking so much *not* like herself that no one recognized her," Jon said, "how are you guys ever going to figure out who she is now, with forty-plus years added on top of it? She could be anyone we've known all our lives."

"But the Reverend might know," Cam said.

"That'd be interesting," Scott said.

"Mo cake!"

Amy's request ended the debate and pulled the attention to her. But she'd already smeared more of Taylor's cake on herself than she'd eaten.

"Speaking of altered appearances," Karis said amid the laughter at the baby, "I think you've had enough cake."

"No! Mo cake!"

Karis got up from her spot on the hearth to take the baby. "Sorry, cake's all gone. And I'd better take you before you get cake all over Taylor, too."

Then she got close enough to see the extent of Amy's mess—cake in her hair, in her ears, up her nose, and even inside the neck of her T-shirt.

"Oh, you definitely need to be stuck in the tub," Karis groaned.

"I don't know," Taylor said with a laugh, "I think she might need to be hosed off."

"I'll get a washcloth," Mara offered as Neily came to help Karis pick crumbs from every wrinkle and crease of Amy and her clothes.

When the baby was finally cleaned up enough to put her coat on, she decided she didn't want to go home and that had to be done amidst her loud protests. Karis did finally manage it, grateful to Boone, who offered then to give Amy an airplane ride while Karis and Luke both got into their jackets. But the airplane play only convinced Amy she really didn't want to leave, making it impossible for Karis to get the spine-arching, wiggling, tantrum-throwing toddler safely into her stroller.

That was when Luke stepped in.

"I'll just carry her," he said, taking Amy, who seemed to make the same decision she had after the blood draws—that Karis was the bad guy. Because once the baby was in Luke's arms, she settled down, stuck her middle fingers in her mouth and glared at her aunt.

Good-nights were said and Amy received kisses from Neily and Mara as well as rump-pats, back rubs and gentle knee-squeezings from her uncles before Karis and Luke finally got out the door.

"Looks like Amy has some fans," Luke observed as they walked the short distance down the street to his house.

"Mmm," Karis agreed. "I'm glad. It's nice for her, even if it does make getting her out of there tougher. They all seem like good aunts and uncles to have," she added, meaning it because the more she saw and learned of her half siblings, the more she liked them. Despite the fact that, when it came to her, she could tell the Northbridge Pratts were still wary.

Not that they didn't have cause, she reminded herself, recalling her own veiled assessment of the house.

She just couldn't help thinking that it would have been so nice if things could have been different.

Then they reached Luke's place and he held open the door for her to push the stroller inside. He followed behind, with Amy looking completely natural there on his hip, as if it was exactly where she belonged.

And the whole thing felt so family-ish to Karis that she suffered a terrible wave of anger at her late sister.

Anger for what Lea had done to Luke, to the real Pratts, to Amy.

Anger for putting her in a situation that showed her how things could be—up the hill and down here, too—if only Lea hadn't already ruined them.

And left Karis in the position of having to make matters even worse.

Chapter Eight

Amy was still peeved at Karis for denying her more cake and more time being fawned over by the Northbridge Pratts when Luke and Karis got her home. The baby wouldn't let Karis take her from Luke, hanging on to his neck every time she tried.

Just as he had at the emergency room, Luke found that funny.

"Sorry," he told Karis with no remorse whatsoever, "you're the heavy again."

"Think so, huh, wise guy? Then who's going to give her her bath and put her to bed? You?"

"Guess I am," he said, surprising her.

Karis motioned to the stairs. "This ought to be something to see."

"I did it for the five weeks I was her father before, you know," Luke said, as he took the challenge and headed for the second floor with Amy.

"Uh-huh," Karis said, following behind and keeping to herself the fact that bathing a newborn was easier than bathing Amy at fifteen months.

"Mo cake?" Amy suggested to him as he took off her coat in the nursery.

"No, no more cake. We're gonna have a bath now," Luke answered as Karis looked on.

"Bubs?" the baby asked.

Luke looked to Karis. "Bubs?" he repeated.

"She wants bubbles."

"Ah." He said to Amy, "You can have all the bubbles you want."

Karis merely smiled.

More cake crumbs flew as Luke undressed the baby, leaving on only her diaper. Then Karis tagged along to the bathroom, where she leaned against the closed door while he set Amy on the floor and filled the tub.

He did test the temperature of the water and put plenty of bubble bath in, but what he failed to do was keep an eye on Amy while he was at it. Or put the toilet seat down.

When he turned to get her, Amy was happily splashing toilet water everywhere.

"No, no, no!" he exclaimed, snatching the baby away from the water and scowling at Karis as she smiled even bigger.

Luke sighed, removed Amy's damp diaper and put her in the bathtub. The fifteen-month-old started splashing all over again, hitting at the bubbles and the water and giving Luke a good sprinkling of both, which sent him rearing back and squinting against the onslaught.

Karis grinned but offered no advice. Instead, she merely enjoyed the spectacle as Luke soaped up a washcloth and used it to bathe Amy while Amy painted his nose, his chin and several spots on his shirt with bubbles, even after he'd repeatedly asked her not to.

"Don't forget her ears," Karis said when he seemed to be.

Amy did not like her ears washed and made that clear, raising a loud—and watery—fuss that ended with the front of Luke's T-shirt wetter still.

That was when he shot Karis a forlorn-looking glance and said, "Hair?"

"There are cake crumbs there, too."

"Mo cake?"

"I don't think you can have cake again until

you're twenty," Luke muttered, making Karis laugh to herself.

Luckily the shampoo was tear-free, because both lathering Amy's curls and rinsing them was fraught with its own perils—suds running down her face, her spitting them out of her mouth when they got that far, and a total lack of cooperation for leaning backward so Luke could rinse her with the water he turned on again for the task.

Ultimately he did get the job done, but by the time he had, he was soaking wet and there were puddles everywhere.

And Amy wasn't any more ready to get out of the bathtub than she had been to leave the Northbridge Pratts' house. She had to be taken out of the water kicking and screaming, which only added to the drenching of both Luke and the bathroom.

Only when he had the baby free of the drink—his hands under her arms, elbows locked to keep her from making contact—did he look around and realize he didn't have a towel ready to dry her.

That was when Karis took pity on him.

She opened the door of the linen closet to her right and got out a clean towel, using it to wrap Amy from behind. Amy had apparently forgiven her, because the baby didn't balk. Karis enfolded her in the towel, taking her from Luke to hold against her own dry V-neck T-shirt and jeans.

"Not quite the same as giving a bath to a five-week-old, is it?" She couldn't resist goading.

Luke looked down at his soaked front. "Apparently not."

"And weren't you supposed to do bedtime, too?" She continued to torment him.

"I think I'll let you handle that while I get out of these wet clothes."

"Mmm-hmm," Karis said, gloating in that small utterance as she got out of the way so he could leave the bathroom.

He did get credit for not hiding out through the entire bedtime ritual, though. By the time Karis had Amy dry and diapered and in her sleeper, Luke joined them in the nursery.

He'd made a quick change into a pair of gray sweatpants and a plain white crew-necked T-shirt, and he looked ready for more. He looked great, since the T-shirt was tight enough to hug his impressive pectorals and biceps, and because even the sweatpants hinted at thick thighs, but still ready for more.

"I'll take over from here," he said.

"Afraid I'll spread the word that you couldn't get the whole job done?" Karis teased.

Luke picked up Amy from the changing table and gave Karis a wicked smile over the baby's curly head. "That's never been said of me before," he countered with a voice full of innuendo.

Amy's eyelids were showing signs of heaviness, so Karis recommended the shortest of her bedtime storybooks. But Luke surprised her yet again by rejecting it. Instead he bypassed the rocking chair and went directly to the crib.

"She likes to be read to," Karis warned in an aside.

Luke ignored Karis and laid the baby on her stomach.

Amy pushed her upper half off the mattress and tossed him a frown over her shoulder to let him know Karis was right. But then he placed one of those massive hands on Amy's back and began a tender massage.

Almost instantly Amy laid her head down, put her middle fingers into her mouth to suck and closed her eyes, as if she'd instinctively recognized the action and responded to it.

"Is this something you did during those first five weeks?" Karis whispered, astonished.

"Every night," Luke whispered back with something in his tone that sounded a little nostalgic and an expression on his face that touched Karis. His expression was sweet and sad and haunting, as if this one moment was what he'd missed most.

It touched Karis so much it made her eyes well up as she pictured the staunch cop with the tiny infant he'd believed to be his daughter. And what he must have suffered to have that so suddenly changed—to be told she *wasn't* his, to have her taken away.

She imagined him coming into this same nursery after that. Standing at that same crib side. And no matter how he'd felt the rest of the time about Lea and what she'd done, here in this room beside an empty crib, he couldn't have felt anything but pain and loss.

His focus was on Amy, so Karis could swipe away the tear that ran down her face and blink back the rest that threatened to fall before he could see them.

She'd barely managed that when Amy stopped sucking her fingers. Her tiny rose-petal lips went slack and there was no doubt she was asleep.

Luke pulled her blanket over her. Karis put her stuffed elephant in the corner of the crib. And they both went silently from the room.

"I need to empty the dishwasher," Karis said, in a hurry to escape the emotions that had come to the surface, and to keep Luke from knowing they had.

"I'll help," he said, and Karis thought he wanted some escape, as well.

Neither of them said anything as they went downstairs and into the kitchen. Only when they got there did Luke say, "The place looks good. You did a lot today."

"It needed a lot," Karis said as they began to unload clean dishes, glasses and utensils.

"Yeah, I've had renters in here since…well, for the last fourteen months."

"Did you rent it furnished?" Karis asked, thinking that would explain why the nursery had been left intact.

"Yeah. I left the whole place the way it was and just walked out of it after Lea left—without cleaning. I guess, when my renters left, they figured it was only fair to leave it the same way."

Karis made a face at that notion. "Yuck."

"Believe me, fourteen months ago I was in no shape to dust or mop."

"Where have you been since then?" she asked.

"Reid and I lived together in a house that was a joint investment on the block behind this one."

"You're real-estate investors?"

"It can be profitable in a college town. In fact, we just bought a second house, but that one was already promised to some other renters when Reid and Chloe got together. Reid and

Chloe needed some privacy, so I didn't have much choice but to move back here. For the time being."

"You're not happy to be back here?"

He shrugged and it was something to see that strong, straight shoulder flex inside the form-fitting knit of his T-shirt.

"Being back here is okay," he conceded. "It's not as bad as I thought it would be. It just needed a cleaning," he summed up.

"Well, now it's had one."

"And I appreciate it," he reiterated.

Karis handed him a stack of cereal bowls that he put into the nearest cupboard. "So if being here isn't as bad as you thought it would be, will you stay?"

"I don't know," he answered, with skepticism in his voice.

"Because you lived here with Lea," Karis guessed.

He shrugged again, but that was his only response. Not committing to more, he said, "I keep doing all the talking about Lea. I think it's your turn. Especially since it occurred to me today, when Cam asked about you, that I still don't know what went on with *you* and your sister."

"Cam asked about me?"

"It's only natural that he'd have some questions." But Luke was apparently not going to be distracted, because he didn't expand on that, returning to what he'd been pursuing before. "You only told me that something Lea did cost you everything you had to keep other people, people who trusted you, from losing their business."

"Is that what I said?" Karis hedged.

"Yes, that's what you said that first night. Almost word for word."

She didn't have a perfectly clear memory of anything about that night except how awful she'd felt. But his claim seemed possible.

"So come on," Luke urged. "Let's have it."

"Dishwasher's empty," Karis said, rather than leaping into an explanation.

"Great, then we can go into the living room, sit and talk," he said, sweeping an arm in the direction of the doorway.

Karis took a deep breath and sighed it out, closing the dishwasher and preceding him from the kitchen into the other room.

Along the way she considered abjectly refusing to tell him what he wanted to know, because it wasn't any of his business and she was disinclined to give him even more reason to think badly of her sister.

But then it occurred to her that maybe she

actually *should* tell him. It might serve as a segue to the time when she would have to let him—and her half siblings—know that she held the deed to the Pratts' house. An explanation for why she needed to do what she needed to do. Possibly, if Luke—and eventually the other Pratts—knew the situation she was in, they might not think as harshly of her as she was afraid they would.

So she sat on the sofa at an angle, facing Luke when he joined her there, and answered his question.

"I told you and the Pratts that I really thought Lea was on the straight and narrow after she and Abe came back to Denver," she began. "And because I did, I pulled some strings and got her a job where I worked."

"Which was where?"

"A small company that's only been in business about two years. You wouldn't have heard of them, but their function was—is—as a middle-man between oil companies and the owners of the mineral rights where the oil companies drill. In a nutshell, the owners of the rights get paid every month from the oil companies, and the company I worked for cut the checks. In order to do that, they had computer access to the royalty accounts of the oil companies."

"Meaning they had access to a whole lot of money."

"Right. Anyway, there are a lot of details about digitalized signatures and blank checks, but the bottom line is that Lea used them to embezzle from my bosses."

Karis had said that quietly, as if it would minimize what her sister had done.

Apparently it didn't work, because Luke's eyebrows arched high. "How much did she embezzle?"

Karis grimaced as she said, "Sixty thousand dollars."

Luke whistled. "Sixty grand?"

Karis nodded.

"That would have gotten her a hefty prison term," he said.

"I know. But I was close to the people I worked for."

"Did they think you were involved? Is that why you don't work for them anymore?"

"No, they didn't think I was involved. They knew me better than that. And they didn't fire me, but the whole thing was awkward and un-comfortable, and emotions were running high for us all, so I couldn't go on working there. But we'd had a good relationship before and, because they liked me and because it was in their best interest, they agreed to let me try to get the money back without calling the police. That's what my father was trying to do when he went to the trailer."

"And then the explosion happened."

Karis nodded a second time.

"Where was the money?"

"In the trailer, according to Abe's and Lea's partner. They'd cashed the checks, used some of the money to rent the trailer and set up the meth lab, but the rest was inside. Incinerated. And after the investigation—"

"Of the embezzlement or the explosion?"

"Both. The explosion forced me to tell the police why my father had gone to the trailer in the first place and why he was fighting with Lea and Abe. That opened up an investigation into the embezzlement, too. But the detectives didn't find any sign of the money being anywhere else—not with the partner and not in a bank account or a safety-deposit box or anywhere. And really, putting it someplace safe wasn't what Lea would have done even with a huge amount of money. The police concluded that the other man was telling the truth when he'd said that whatever was left of the sixty thousand—"

"Went up in smoke."

"Poof."

Luke's eyebrows rose again. He shook his head and glanced off in the distance as if letting it all sink in. "And I thought your sister had done damage here."

Karis didn't comment on that.

"Then what?" he asked.

"Then it was just a matter of dealing with the fallout."

"Lea, Abe and your father were gone and so was the money, but the company you worked for was still out sixty thousand dollars—that was the fallout," Luke surmised.

"Exactly. The company I worked for had insurance that would have covered them, but to make a claim would have cost them years of sky-high premiums. Worse than that, they— and I—knew that if they filed a claim, their clients would find out what had happened and the business they were just beginning to build would be sunk. Even though, after the fact, they put in safeguards to prevent anything like this from happening again, they would have lost the accounts they had and there was no way they'd get anyone else to hire them. They would have been through."

"And without putting in an insurance claim, they were liable for the sixty thousand themselves."

"Every penny of it. Which they didn't have. But coming up with the sixty thousand was the only way to salvage what Lea had done." Karis paused, took another breath and said, "So I promised to pay it."

"With everything you owned," Luke concluded.

"Not that I *owned* much. I was only renting an apartment. I gave that up and got the damage deposit back. I sold everything except my clothes and my car. I cashed in the retirement fund I had and closed out my checking and savings accounts. I took cash advances on credit cards. I gave them everything I could scrape up."

"Which was how much?"

"Thirty-three thousand, one hundred and thirty-seven dollars."

"A lot. But still a long way from sixty."

Karis nodded once more.

"And you still have to come up with the rest."

"For now my former employers have done that with their own savings and a short-term loan so they could cover up what happened and buy me some time."

"Time you used to come to Northbridge."

She knew what he was thinking and she wouldn't leave him with those thoughts.

"I inherited something from my father," she said.

"You did? You alone?"

"Me, alone. Not that he had much—he was renting, too. There was his car, a few thousand in a bank account and a small life-insurance policy. All of that went into the thirty-three I paid off the debt. But there was one other thing and, yes, he had a legal and binding will that left everything there was to me."

"Not to *any* of his other kids?"

"No. I know he didn't put Lea in the will, because he was afraid anything she got her hands on wouldn't be used wisely. Besides, he also knew that I always took care of her when she needed anything so whatever he left to me would sift down to her anyway. But I don't understand why he ignored his kids here."

Especially when the only real thing of value that he'd owned was *their* house.

"It's lousy," Karis added. "But that's what he did."

"And the *one other thing* he left you?"

Should she tell him?

She considered it.

Should she tell him that the one other thing was the Pratts' house, and that she was going to have to borrow against it to get the rest of the money? That she was going to put a mortgage on a place she actually had no right to? A place where other people lived? A place that other people believed was theirs and theirs alone, free and clear of debt?

She couldn't.

In the end, she just couldn't tell Luke, not any more than she'd been able to tell her half siblings.

So in answer to his inquiry about the one other thing her father had left her, she did some beating around the bush.

"It's just sort of another iron in the fire that I can use."

"Sort of another iron in the fire..." Luke repeated. "What is this, a riddle? Did he leave you something you're going to blackmail someone with or something?"

Karis laughed. "No, it's nothing like that. It's legitimate and no one will get hurt by it." Although no one was going to be thrilled with it either.

He frowned at her. "Meaning?"

Karis raised her chin defiantly. "Meaning that I can see you're on the alert again, thinking I've come here to hit you or the real Pratts for money," she added with mock intrigue in her tone, "or to blackmail someone. But I haven't. That isn't how I'm going to get out of this, so you can put down your antennae."

That brought an instant grin to his face and it took her a moment to realize that he'd heard a double entendre in it.

And even though Karis hadn't intended anything lascivious, she didn't regret having inadvertently lightened the tone.

"So," he said, "you were working somewhere you liked, with people you cared about. You helped your sister out by getting her a job and she put you in this position. That stinks."

Karis laughed again. "I can't argue with that. It's been pretty awful."

He was angled on the sofa facing her, too, one arm stretched along the top of the sofa back, shaking his head in censure of her sister, she was sure. But for once he didn't use what she'd told him to support his own case against Lea. Instead he said wryly, "Okay, you win—sixty thousand dollars embezzled, a meth lab in a trailer, an explosion, three deaths. I can't compete."

"Was it a contest?"

"Apparently not. No wonder you don't think what she did here was such a big deal."

"I didn't say that," Karis insisted. "I'm sorry for what Lea did here. To you and to the Pratts.

It was no less rotten because she came home and did what she did there. She was a train wreck."

"But she was still your sister—I know, I know," he said, anticipating the end of her sentence.

Karis merely shrugged.

Luke studied her with piercing eyes for a long moment. "Are you this loyal to everyone?" he asked.

"Is that a bad thing?"

"I don't know if it's been such a good thing for you, but it's lucky for a lot of other people," he said quietly.

Karis didn't know what to say to that, so she didn't say anything. It didn't seem to matter though, because something in the air between them was changing and she just let his gaze hold hers as he looked into her eyes as if he were trying to see beyond the surface. As if maybe, for the first time, he *was* seeing beyond the surface. Or at least, beyond his own preconceived idea of who and what she was.

And for no reason Karis could explain, she was suddenly thinking about the kiss he'd planted on her in the nursery before the football game. About how it was supposed to have closed some kind of window on that inclination in them both. About how the window didn't seem closed in her at all, because she couldn't think about anything but how terrific the kiss had been and how much she wished he would kiss her again. Right then. Even though she told herself and told herself and told herself no…

Luke shook his head and she wasn't sure why.

Was their conversation still on his mind? Or was he reading hers and telling her he wasn't going to kiss her?

Or was he thinking the way she was, that they'd been naive to believe the kiss in the nursery had put anything behind them?

She thought the last possibility was the likeliest when he reached a single index finger to sweep her hair away from her brow, to smooth it behind her ear and slide his hand through it to the back of her head. When he leaned forward at the same time, he gently pulling her to meet him halfway and finding her mouth with his.

And even though hours had gone by since the other kiss, this one picked up where it had left off. And went from there.

Lips were parted when they met, soft but sure and steady and unsurprised. Karis raised a hand of her own to Luke's chest, the chest that was barely contained in the thin T-shirt he'd changed into. The chest that was warm and solid and wonderful to touch.

His free hand came to the side of her face, caressing it with the feather-light stroke of his thumb as his lips parted more and his tongue came to explore the maiden route into hers.

Karis put up no obstacles. She opened the way, sending her tongue as a welcoming committee. Tip to tip, they said hello in a velvety greeting that went straight to play. Sexy, sensuous play. Circles and spirals and twists and turns that all brought Karis closer to Luke, Luke closer to Karis.

Mouths opened wider and somehow Karis's arms found a path around Luke. Somehow her hands were splayed against his broad, muscular back, reveling in the feel of the power and pure mass and heat of him. Somehow her breasts, with their nipples tight nuggets, nudged against the chest she'd only moments before felt beneath her palm.

His arms were around her, too. A ring of muscles, that wrapped her in a tender strength and held her as the weight of that kiss that grew deeper and deeper, began to bend her backward.

Why that brought her more to her senses was as much a mystery as how this had started in the first place. But as quickly as it had, Karis remembered where she was and who she was with and the situation she was in. She knew she had to stop this, even though there wasn't any part of her that wanted to.

Her tongue did a retreat at the same moment she withdrew her arms from around him and put her hands against his chest again, this time pushing—however feebly.

Luke got the message. He ended the kiss and eased up on his hold of her. He sat straighter, leaving her to rebalance, regroup and regret that he was gone.

"History repeating itself?" he asked, referring to what they'd said about the earlier kiss making their curiosity a thing of the past.

"Something repeating itself," Karis answered.

"And it wasn't supposed to," he said, as if reluctantly reminding himself.

"That was my understanding."

"Not so easy," he confessed.

"No," she agreed, unable to keep the hint of a smile from her lips when she saw the hint of one on his.

"We'll try harder?"

He posed that as a question and Karis thought that if she said they didn't have to, he might just take her back into his arms and kiss her all over again.

And it was tempting.

Oh, was it tempting!

But the situation was already full of the fallout that her sister had left for each of them. So that wasn't what she said.

"We'd probably better try harder."

Luke nodded, but the sigh he breathed said he might have preferred it if she'd disagreed with the last suggestion and given the go-ahead instead.

Still, he accepted her decision and stood, clearly to put some distance between them. "Best behavior from now on?"

"Okay," she said, without much conviction, because it wasn't as if she hadn't been on her best behavior already. Or that she thought he hadn't been. It was more that something had overtaken them and she didn't know if it had anything to do with how they behaved.

"I have to work tomorrow until two in the afternoon," Luke informed her. "I thought maybe we could go get Amy a Halloween costume when I come home and let her do some trick-or-treating tomorrow night. The whole town gets in on the act. I think you'd both like it."

"That sounds fun," Karis said, as if she hadn't forgotten that the next day was Halloween. In truth, Amy was too young for it to matter. But it occurred to her that the holiday might offer a distraction from the attraction that seemed to take over when they least expected it to, a distraction they apparently needed.

"Great," Luke said. "I think I'll go up and shower now, try to get some sleep. You?"

"Soon. I'll turn the lights off down here in a minute and go up," Karis said, worried that if they went anywhere near the bedrooms together things might start again.

"I'll say good-night then," Luke said.

"Good night," Karis answered.

Her back was to the entryway and the staircase and she didn't turn to watch him go. But it required some willpower not to, and she listened to every step, every creak of the wood, knowing exactly when he went into his room, when he closed his door, when he got into the shower.

She couldn't help wondering if the shower he was taking was warm or cold.

Because, while she'd never tried taking a cold one to cool the aftereffects of something like the kiss they'd just shared, it seemed as if maybe she should test it out now.

Now, when she was definitely feeling hot and bothered and nowhere near relaxed enough to sleep.

Now, when all she could think about was following him up the stairs, into his room, into his shower…

Stop it! she silently shrieked at herself.

But regardless of how firmly, how fiercely she tried to put a halt to her thoughts of Luke, she just couldn't.

Not with the image of him still so vividly in her mind. With the clean scent, the essence of him, still a presence in the air all around her.

And certainly not after two powerhouse kisses in one day that had only left her wishing for more.

Chapter Nine

"**W**ere you just on the phone with Denver PD?"

Luke had only been in the office for an hour on Tuesday morning when he'd made the call Cam was referring to. Their desks faced each other and Luke hadn't worried about privacy because he'd figured he was going to end up talking to Cam about it anyway.

"I was. With the lead detective who handled the explosion."

"Did you call Denver or did Denver call you?" Cam asked, because he'd been away from his desk getting coffee at the time.

"I called them," Luke answered, leaning back in his chair.

"How come?"

Luke repeated all that Karis had told him the night before about the embezzlement and about the debt she was carrying.

"When I talked to the Denver guy before I didn't know any of this and just asked about the explosion and the deaths. That was all we got into. So I called back to check out the rest of it."

"Not too trusting of our girl?" Cam said.

Luke shrugged. "Better safe than sorry. After her sister."

Cam nodded his agreement. "What did the Denver guy say?"

"He verified this part, too."

"Our money wasn't enough for Lea. She went back there and took sixty thousand on top of it a year later?"

"That's the report."

"And she took it from the place she and Karis both worked?"

"Right."

"Man…" Cam shook his head in amazement. "There was just nothing she wouldn't do, was there?"

"Did you have a doubt?"

"I shouldn't have," Cam said. Then he frowned. "Any chance Karis was involved?"

"The word on that is no, she wasn't," Luke

answered, trying not to be as pleased as he was by that. "In fact, the owners of the business were so sure she wasn't involved or to blame that they defended her when they were questioned about whether or not they thought she should be charged with complicity. They even denied the opportunity to sue her for damages, which I guess some lawyer tried to get them to do. They were confident Karis would come through with her promise to repay the money."

"And she says she *has* paid over half of it?"

"I told the detective she was claiming that and he said it was true," Luke confirmed. "He said he'd kept an eye on her, on her finances, on what she's been up to these last six weeks—"

"In case she had the sixty grand herself and might lead them to it," Cam guessed.

"I'm sure."

"And?"

"And all she's done is what she told me she did—moved out of her apartment, sold everything she could, closed her bank accounts, took cash advances on credit cards, and paid every penny she could lay her hands on to her former employers."

"So no lies, huh?" Cam mused.

"Not so far," Luke allowed, worried about letting down his guard at all, let alone too fast.

At least when he wasn't with her. When he was with her? That was a whole different story.

"What about the rest of the sixty? Did she say how she was going to come up with that?" Cam asked.

Luke hadn't been sure whether or not to tell his friend about the fact that Karis was the only one of the Pratt offspring to be mentioned in their mutual father's will. But since he couldn't stanch all of his suspicions about her when he *wasn't* with her, he opted to.

"I'm sorry to be the one to tell you," he said when he had.

Cam didn't seem disturbed by the news. "Dear old Dad hadn't bothered with any of us since three months after the triplets were born—that's twenty-nine years ago. It's no wonder he didn't put us in his will. We were strangers to him—he was a stranger to us. But what does that have to do with how Karis might come up with the rest of the money to pay back her former employers?" Cam asked, returning to his original question.

Luke hoped Cam was as detached as he sounded. "She said she liquidated everything of his, too. That that had all gone into what she repaid. But for the rest of it, she said she had another iron in the fire."

Luke went on to tell Cam that portion of what he and Karis had talked about the night before.

"You don't have any idea what she was talking about?"

"No. And she skirted it."

"Which sounds an alarm."

Luke shrugged. "I don't know if it should or not. It could be that she just figured it wasn't any of my business."

"Or it could be that it's underhanded. Or worse," Cam contended.

It wasn't altogether easy for Luke to give Karis the benefit of the doubt. Apparently it was even more difficult for Cam, who then said, "And she's here in Northbridge. Is that because this is where her other iron in the fire is?"

"I can't say that hasn't occurred to me, too," Luke confessed somewhat unwillingly.

"And if the other iron in the fire *is* here, is it you or us?" Cam continued, postulating the way they had innumerable times when they'd investigated cases that had crossed their desks.

"It could be nothing to do with anyone here." Luke felt a need to present the flip side of the coin rather than gang up on Karis. "Maybe she has some kind of family heirloom from her mother that she doesn't want to part with. Maybe she hoped she wouldn't have to but is just now facing the fact that she does, that she's going to have to auction it off on eBay or something."

"Or she has something else her sister stole that she's going to try to sell."

"That doesn't fit," Luke said, knowing he was increasingly coming to Karis's defense but unable to help himself. "She's sold off her own things to repay what Lea took from their employers. I don't think she'd use something else Lea swiped to come up with the rest of it. I think she'd be more likely to give back anything Lea wrongfully got her hands on."

"I don't know. I haven't seen a check for what her sister lied to get out of us here," Cam said.

The comment rubbed Luke wrong, something that had never happened when they were doing this kind of back-and-forth over a case.

Even though he recognized that his annoyance might be connected to his attraction to Karis, he was still compelled to say, "Jeez, cut her a little slack! She's down to living in her car to keep people from losing their livelihood because of what Lea took from them. She didn't even know about what Lea had conned out of you guys until I told her a few days ago. And as lousy as it is that Lea did it at all, none of you are in trouble for the money you pitched in. But

you're ticked off because she hasn't sold blood
to give you something back?"

"Whoa! Did I touch a nerve?"

"I'm just saying that so far we've had confirmation for everything she's said. She's doing a
whole lot more than most people would do to
make up for inflicting Lea on her employers, so
it doesn't follow that her other iron in the fire
is illegal or unethical."

Cam didn't look convinced. "Yeah? Talk to
me when you find out Amy *is* yours and Karis
holds her for ransom."

"Come on," Luke said, as if his friend was out
of his mind to even suggest something like that.

"I'm just saying I'm not convinced that we
don't have to worry about her or about her being
here or what her other iron in the fire is. And I
mean *we* as in you—" he punctuated that with a
finger extended toward Luke "—because of Amy.
And us—" a thumb went to his chest "—as in the
left-behind-Pratts because of who-knows-what."

"I honestly don't know how her iron in the
fire could have anything to do with me or with
you all," Luke persisted.

"Even so, I think we all need to be on the alert."

"Granted," Luke conceded. "But I don't
think we need to be unfair to her in the
process. I've kept my eye on her, along with

checking up on her twice now. And so far she's squeaky clean. Let's at least give her points for that."

"Points, but not the whole game. And maybe you'd better look out if I can get your back up this easily over her," Cam added, pushing himself away from his desk to stand. "I'm due out at the search site. I'll see you later."

Cam left Luke alone in the office, but Luke didn't plunge into the paperwork he had waiting in front of him. Instead he thought about how the conversation with his friend had ended up.

And wondered what the hell was going on with him when it came to Karis.

Why did he keep starting out in one place with her—or with anything that involved her— and ending up in another place? A place he shouldn't end up?

He'd begun the conversation with Cam wanting to keep his guard up.

He'd ended it not only defending Karis, but striking out at Cam.

Just the way he'd started out this week being wary of her and of her motives and of why she was here at all.

And ended up kissing her yesterday.

Twice!

And worse than that, if she hadn't pushed

him away the second time last night, he might have gone and done more than kiss her.

He really had to watch himself.

Maybe more than he had to watch her.

But keeping himself in check was getting progressively harder to do.

And not only because the more he was with her, the more he was attracted to her. There was also some validity in what he'd said to Cam. She *had* been straight with them. So far, everything she'd said had been verified. And there was nothing suspicious or questionable about anything she was doing. If she were a suspect in a crime that would have allowed them to ease up on her.

Ease up on her, not kiss her...

But as much as he wanted to deny it, Karis was a hard person not to like.

He recalled telling himself early on, when his attraction to her had initially come to life, that he'd push thoughts of her away with bad memories of Lea. That there was no repellant stronger than that.

But apparently he'd been wrong. Because when he was with Karis—even when they were talking about Lea—he still saw Karis in her own light.

And it was such a nice, warm glow of a light....

But that didn't mean he could forget about what—about who—had come before her and that she and Lea had the same roots. And maybe the same motives, too. It didn't mean he could close his eyes to the possibility that Karis was there to pass off Amy onto him whether or not he was her father. It didn't mean he could be sure she wasn't there to take him and the other Pratts to the cleaners somehow. Because he couldn't be sure. And so he couldn't forget or close his eyes to anything.

Cam was right. She got points for her honesty, but that didn't win her the whole game. They all still needed to be on the alert with her.

And not alert to what he'd been alert to, Luke told himself. Like how damn adorable she looked when she cocked her head to one side. Like the fact that, to him, her voice sounded as sweet as heated maple syrup on pancakes when he heard it first thing in the morning. Like the way she smelled all clean and faintly flowery. Like the way her hair waved around her face in wisps. Like the way her breasts seemed as if they might fit into the palms of his hands...

Luke snapped himself out of his reverie, again disgusted with himself for not staying on track and grateful no one had come into the office and caught him fantasizing on duty.

Oh yeah, Cam had definitely known what he was talking about when he'd advised him to look out.

And Luke knew that was exactly what he had to do. From now on, he couldn't give an inch where Karis was concerned. He had to be vigilant in looking for signs of what her other iron in the fire might be, for signs that she posed a threat to him or to anyone else he knew.

And he had to be extra vigilant in resisting the weakness he had for her.

Which meant no more kissing.

No more anything.

And he was determined to stick to that.

He swore it.

Then he glanced at the clock on the side wall. Before he even realized what he was doing, he was counting how long it would be before he got to go home to Karis.

Karis had never been anyplace for Halloween where so many people were as enthusiastic about celebrating the holiday as the population of Northbridge.

She'd had an idea that the small town went all out, when she, Luke and Amy shopped for Amy's costume that afternoon. There was so much activity that she could tell things were gearing up for an event. But when she saw the results after dark Tuesday evening as she and Luke walked along Main Street with Amy in her stroller, Karis still couldn't quite believe her eyes.

Not only were more people in elaborate costume than weren't, the entire town itself had been dressed up for the festivities.

Jack-o'-lantern lights were strung from pole lamp to pole lamp, from one end of Main to the other. The shops were all open, though not for business, only so owners and operators could pass out candy and confections to the trick-or-treaters who had no need to go house to house when the best goodies were being given there.

Besides the window decorations that had been on display since Karis arrived, tonight there were expertly carved pumpkins blazing with candles in front of every structure. There were ghosts, goblins, scarecrows, skeletons and wart-nosed witches dancing from bare tree branches whenever a breeze took them. There were ornamental black cats climbing in and out of the flower boxes around the streetlights. There were eerie sounds being piped into the thoroughfare, and mannequins turned into comical monsters stood sentry here and there.

And it all led to the Town Square, where even more was going on. Booths were set up selling food or offering Halloween games. Contests and races were being held. A huge tent that looked like a black circus tent had been erected as a haunted house. The gazebo was aglow with tiny white and orange lights, and on its platform were barrels full of apples to be bobbed for.

And the costumes!

Karis had thought the handmade fluffy pink bunny suit that Amy had picked out herself was something to see. But that and what most of the kids wore couldn't compare to the outfits of the adults. There was a Robin Hood complete with tights, bow and arrow. There was someone in a full suit of armor. Dracula really did look like a count and had vampire teeth that appeared real. Frankenstein was every bit of eight feet tall. Guesses were being made as to who was in the giant soup can. The werewolf was so intimidating he frightened several of the kids, but Amy loved him—possibly because she sensed that he was her Uncle Boone. And person after person caused Karis to feel underdressed in her jeans, navy-blue turtleneck sweater and peacoat.

"Does this go on every year?" she asked Luke, as she watched Dorothy from the *Wizard of Oz* being followed by someone dressed as a Christmas tree all lit up, tinseled and ornamented, with his gold-painted face the center of the star on top.

"Every year," Luke said. He shook hands with Abraham Lincoln and waved at Darth Vader in complete regalia several feet away.

"Then you should be ashamed of yourself for not dressing up, too," Karis chastised, though she had no complaint with the jeans, yellow polo sweater and leather jacket he had on. In fact, he looked tremendous in the clothes that fit him well enough to hint at the powerfully fine body underneath them without being too tight or showy. But she was trying not to notice that in a renewed attempt to temper what had led to kissing the previous day.

"I just like to see everybody else," he informed her, pointing out the double-headed space alien headed their way.

The corpse bride accompanying the alien was Neily, and Mara—as the tooth fairy—was behind them.

"Hey, Jon," Luke said, without needing to be told who the space alien was.

"Happy Halloween," Jon greeted from inside the mask.

"You knew who he was?" Karis asked.

"He wears the same thing year after year," Neily tattled.

The three local Pratts fussed over Amy and dropped treats into her plastic pumpkin before offering to stay with her if Luke and Karis wanted to go through the haunted house.

"I don't know," Karis said before Luke could give his answer. "I don't like to be scared."

"Chicken," he accused and challenged at once. "How scary do you think it can be? This is Northbridge. And it's in a tent."

"A black tent," Karis pointed out, unsure if he was lying to lure her.

"I think you can handle it," Jon said. "Even kids are going in."

But not small kids, Karis noted.

Still, she didn't want to appear weak and neurotic to Luke or to her half siblings, so she conceded and left Amy with her costumed aunts and uncle while she and Luke made their way to the haunted-house tent.

A ghoul was the doorman and he made sure a few minutes separated groups he admitted inside. Since there were teenagers in front and behind them in line who wanted to be together, Karis and Luke were sent in on their own.

The inside of the tent was lit only sparingly in black light, which made Luke's perfect teeth look all the whiter when he smiled and said, "Want me to hold your hand?"

What his touch stirred in her seemed more unsettling than anything she could encounter in the haunted house, so Karis rolled her eyes and said, "Because *you're* scared?"

His smile turned into a grin almost as broad as the *Alice In Wonderland* Cheshire cat perched to one side of the entrance. "Don't say I didn't offer."

Dangling spiders and webs were in abundance at the start as they made their way through the winding passage they were to walk along. A bony hand reached out to them from inside a curtain. They passed a spooky fortune-teller, her recorded voice predicting terror to come, and moved on to an old wooden coffin. The top opened just as they neared it so the corpse inside—who looked remarkably like Taylor—could sit up and moan.

A witch mixed a smoking, bubbling concoction in another section, beckoning onlookers to come closer, as if she would push them into the pot to add to her brew. Then a hunchbacked apothecary offered jars of eyeballs and lizard guts for only a quarter.

"You're right, this is a Northbridge-style haunted house—it's more cute than scary," Karis whispered to Luke as they moved among the eerie sound effects of creaking doors, shattering glass, ghostly mutterings and female shrieks of horror.

Goblins dropped down from above, forcing them to duck underneath them. In the distance a headless man dashed across the makeshift corridor carrying his noggin under his arm, and skeletons dined in another section, their bones bleached in the black light as a gnarl-handed maid served them, oblivious to the ax embedded in her skull.

By then Karis thought she had the measure of the haunted house and that there wouldn't be anything too gruesome or terrifying to come, so she relaxed.

And about the time she did, someone in a hockey mask wielding a chain saw jumped out of the blackest of shadows and scared her right into Luke's arms.

Not that he'd been waiting for it. She couldn't be sure, but she thought he'd taken a jolt, too. But the pure force of Karis's rebound crashed her into him and he had to catch her.

He recovered before she did and said, "Uh, hello," just as the chain saw massacre receded into the shadows again.

Karis's back was against his chest, his arms were around her middle. Even in her fright, it registered as a good feeling. A really good feeling—warm and solid and comforting.

A feeling she wasn't eager to lose.

And maybe neither was he, because he was late in letting go of her.

But he did, finally, making sure she was steady on her feet first.

"Okay, not so cute," she grumbled, repealing her earlier judgment and hoping he thought her voice was affected by the fright and not by having just rubbed up against him, which was, in fact, the cause.

"It wouldn't be Halloween without at least one scare," he said, his own tone deeper than it had been before.

"Did you know that was coming?"

"I knew it would happen somewhere in here."

"Will it happen again?"

"No, it's one to a customer."

Again Karis wasn't sure whether he was lying and, just in case he was, she made him walk ahead of her the rest of the way.

But nothing else unexpected happened. They reached the end of the line and came out of the tent to find Amy, Neily and Mara waiting for them.

There were no more frights the remainder of the evening, either. Instead, it was just plain fun. With Mara and Neily along, they all ate caramel apples, watched the mock swordfight between two knights, saw the parade of costumes and the awarding of the prizes for the best of them. They cheered on the apple bobbers and got to sample the taffy after the taffy pull.

Amy spent part of the time in her stroller with one of her bunny ears in her mouth, and part of the time being carried. But no matter where she was, she was enthralled with everything going on around her.

She was a big draw herself, too. Apparently most of the town had met her during her first five weeks of life, and those who hadn't already seen her again, sought her out tonight. All of them—and everyone else who passed by her—dropped goodies into her plastic pumpkin despite the fact that she hadn't quite mastered saying "trick or treat." Nor did she seem to comprehend why they were doing that.

The festivities wrapped up around ten o'clock, and by then Amy was asleep in her stroller for the walk back to Luke's house once Mara and Neily had said good-night and left them.

There were other people wandering back to their homes, too, and Karis marveled at their costumes all the way to Luke's front door.

Once they were inside again, though, Halloween seemed to end. Karis said, "I really had a good time. Thanks for taking us."

Luke shrugged. "We couldn't miss it," he said.

It also seemed like the time to say good-night, but before Karis had convinced herself to do what she didn't feel inclined to do, Luke said, "I'm hungry for something that *isn't* sweet. How about I make a couple of sand-wiches while you put Amy to bed and you can balance out some of those candy bars you kept sneaking from her pumpkin?"

Karis *had* eaten more than her quota of chocolate, and something savory—and salty—was an appealing thought. Especially if it meant they would have a little time alone—forbidden though she knew that should be after the two kisses the previous day.

"Sounds good," she agreed, ignoring the fact that it would be so much smarter to go up to bed herself and actually make it through the entire day without tempting fate.

But when Luke said, "I'll meet you in the kitchen then," Karis said, "Okay."

They'd both removed their coats and hung them on the hall tree, so Karis unstrapped the sleeping baby, took her out of the stroller and headed for the stairs as Luke went to the kitchen.

The kitchen—that was where she was supposed to meet him, she reminded herself.

The kitchen seemed like safe territory—

cooking, eating, cleaning and talking, that's all
that ever went on there. There wouldn't be any
sitting on the sofa or sitting in front of a fire. There
wouldn't be any standing face-to-face, coming
closer and closer together as if she were a magnet
and he were metal. And certainly no one would
jump out at them and fling her into his arms.

So surely they couldn't get into trouble there,
she reasoned. They would just be two people
having a snack—nothing more, nothing less,
nothing in the least bit romantic.

The kitchen.

It was okay to continue this evening as long
as they stayed in the kitchen, she told herself.

And if she had to push away fantasies of
Luke clearing the table with one swipe of a
powerful arm and making mad, passionate love
to her right there?

Fantasies weren't actions.

And she just needed not to act on the fantasy.

Chapter Ten

"Here's what we have—turkey, ham, two cheeses, tomato, avocado slices and sprouts on French bread with my secret blend of herbed mayo and Italian salad dressing. And potato chips."

That was how Luke greeted Karis when she met him in the kitchen after putting Amy to bed.

"Holy cow!" Karis said, unable not to admire the picture of the big, handsome man so pleased with himself and his concoction. "I could use a glass of water to go with it. Can I get you a drink, too?"

"Water," Luke answered as he sliced the

sandwich he'd made by cutting a half-loaf of bread lengthwise down the middle, hollowing out some of the soft inside, filling the center with a variety of meats, cheeses, vegetables and condiments, and then replacing the top of the bread.

They made it to the table at the same time and settled across from each other with paper plates and napkins in front of them. Luke proudly served her the first slice of sandwich, put two on his own plate, and poured chips out of the bag to join Karis's snack before his own.

All the while, she watched him, appreciating his smoothly rugged features, his short, neat, sable-colored hair, his green eyes, and that lean body hugged to droolable perfection by his yellow polo shirt.

"Dig in," he advised.

There's only safety in the kitchen if you stop ogling him, she told herself, forcing her attention down to her plate while she tried to swallow the rise of attraction once more.

The sandwich was plump with meat, cheeses and produce, spilling sprouts in every direction, and seeing it caused Karis to smile.

"Sprouts, huh?" she said, goading him slightly.

"Alfalfa. They're good for you and they're crunchy and earthy tasting on a hoagie."

Karis nodded, struck again by what had

occurred to her when she'd initially set eyes on him—well, once she'd overcome her shock at how gorgeous he was. It struck her again that this man was unlike the other men her sister had been attracted to. And it also struck her that the more she got to know him, the more odd it seemed that he'd gone for Lea.

"What?" he said, interrupting her musings and making her realize that, rather than tasting the sandwich, she was staring at him. "Do you hate sprouts? Or is something else not to your liking?"

Not in the sandwich and not in him. That was part of the problem when it came to resisting him. And also part of why she'd been lost in her own curiosity.

"No, I like sprouts, and the whole sandwich looks great. I was just thinking...wondering, I guess..."

She wasn't sure how to put it.

She finally decided on, "I was wondering how you and Lea got together? Somehow it doesn't seem like you would have been each other's type."

"I'm not talking until you eat."

She hadn't noticed that he was waiting for her before he took a bite himself. So she tasted his accomplishment, complimented him profusely, and only after she had did he dig into his portion of the sandwich and answer her question.

"I met Lea when she came speeding into town—literally, she was going eighty-one miles an hour in the fifty-five zone just outside of Northbridge. I pulled her over to give her a ticket."

"Should I be afraid to ask how she got out of it?"

"Apologies and promises to slow down and flirting and, yes, I'm only human and she was blond and pretty and sexy and I was hit with something I'd never been hit with before. I fell head over heels just about on the spot."

Karis knew her eyebrows had arched high. "Oh," she said, hating that there was a forlorn note in her voice. But it was difficult to suppress it in view of coming face-to-face once again in her life with a sense of paling by comparison to her flashier, wilder, more confident, completely uninhibited sister.

"And in whatever madness had overtaken me—and I *do* consider it some kind of temporary insanity—" Luke went on. "I let myself be persuaded to marry her on what she made seem like a whim. Four days later."

"Four days?" Karis repeated, after nearly choking on surprise and sandwich.

"See? I told you, I had to have been out of my mind. But yeah, four days."

Karis took a drink of water, munched a chip, and said, "So getting married was Lea's idea?"

Luke nodded confirmation while he washed down some of his own food. "We'd been on a picnic and from early in the afternoon to late at night she'd been bringing me beer after beer. I can't even tell you how many I must have had but I was feeling no pain when she started acting like she'd just had a sudden notion that we should do something nutty—like elope. And I fell for it. I was too drunk to drive but she wasn't. We got in the car, went to Billings, and that's all she wrote."

"But you don't think eloping was a sudden notion?"

"I didn't once I found out Amy wasn't mine. Then I started thinking Amy hadn't been a preemie, and that Lea had been pregnant when she got here. By then it was clear that nothing she'd said about why she'd come to town or about me was true, so yes, it followed that she'd been putting on an act when she got the whim to marry me. I figured the real father of her baby hadn't wanted anything to do with her and I was the sap she got to take his place. Until five weeks after Amy was born, when they must have made up and *Abe* was ready to take over."

Karis wondered if Luke would ever shake the bitterness he so obviously felt.

"Had you been married before?" she asked.

"No. I hadn't even had many serious romances beyond the adolescent crushes everybody goes through."

"Really?" Karis said. She didn't find it easy to believe that anyone who looked like he did hadn't had legions of women flocking to him.

"Affairs of the heart can be tough to come by in a small town. Sometimes those adolescent crushes turn into the real thing and people couple-up for good from young ages. Sometimes—like for me—the women you know as adults are the same girls you grew up with, and since those adolescent crushes didn't turn into the real thing, they all just seem like sisters to you. There have been a few new people who've come into town that I've gotten to know, but nothing panned out—"

"And then there was Lea," Karis finished for him.

"And then there was Lea. Who acted as if she'd buzzed in to look up the half siblings she'd never met and happened to fall instantly in love with me in the process."

"Are you so sure it was an act?"

He shrugged. "Believe me, my ego would like to think it wasn't, but what are the odds?"

Karis thought they were pretty good if the

main factor was his appeal. But she couldn't offer any information because Lea hadn't given her anything to go on. Lea had disappeared without a word and waited until after Amy's birth to send the single message Karis had received from her. She'd sent a note telling Karis she was married and had had a baby. Period. No details. And when she'd returned to Denver, she'd avoided the subject of Northbridge and what had gone on here.

So rather than contributing anything, Karis said, "What about the ten months you were married? Did it seem as if she was just using you?"

"No, I can't say it seemed as if she was just using me."

"So maybe she wasn't. Did she work at the marriage?"

A second shrug. "Work at it? Lea didn't work at anything. Plus she was pregnant right out of the gate so I didn't expect her to be a superhousewife. And she seemed to be thrilled that we were going to have a baby and since I was, too, I bought it all."

"But you believe it was an act?"

"I'm not saying she didn't put on a *good* act—with me and with the Pratts. And she was so different from anyone else we knew—

wilder, more fun-loving, more free-spirited, lighter, breezier—we all thought she was a breath of fresh air. At least until Amy was born."

"And then?" Karis asked, finished with her food but not with her yen to know about Luke's relationship with her sister.

"Things—Lea—changed after Amy was born. Her whole personality changed. She was moody. Sullen. Angry. Reid said it was postpartum depression."

"You didn't think so?" Karis said, interpreting his tone.

"I wanted to think so. Just like I wanted to believe when I caught her making late-night, secretive phone calls that they really were to girlfriends in Denver. Just like I wanted to believe that when I caught her rifling through the Pratts' drawers after a dinner we had there that she really was just searching for a tissue. Just like I wanted to believe when I caught her popping pills that they really were just an herbal remedy she'd ordered from a catalog."

"You wanted to believe it all but you didn't?"

"I wanted to believe it all so I did. Even though—"

"Even though something kind of ate at you that said things weren't what Lea claimed," Karis said, understanding, because that was always how her sister's early retreats back into drugs had been for her. She hadn't wanted to think the worst so she'd tried to believe Lea's excuses for things that had seemed questionable.

"Yes, I wanted to believe it all so I did, even though something ate at me that said I shouldn't. Something I ended up wishing I'd paid more attention to when I found out I had reason to doubt her."

"What about Amy?" Karis asked then. "Was there anything that made you think she might not be yours?"

"No, nothing," he said, as if he were disgusted with himself because it hadn't. "Being Amy's dad was honestly something I never questioned. Not for a minute. I just thought—and so did everyone else—that she was born at eight months. She was small, only five pounds, six ounces, so it seemed reasonable that she hadn't gone to full term. That she was mine. Then, when Lea dropped the bomb that she *wasn't* mine, I knew it was possible Lea could have been pregnant before I ever met her and Amy had just had a low birth weight at full term."

"Or she really could have been an early-term baby," Karis said.

Luke didn't respond one way or another.

"How was Lea with Amy during those five weeks?" Karis inquired.

"Not very interested. Impatient with the demands of a newborn. Frustrated. Irritated."

Signs Karis knew indicated that Lea was itching to be back on drugs and not that she didn't care about Amy.

"But again," Luke continued, "Reid said those could all be the depression. So I took almost total care of Amy when I was off duty and my mother came in to help when I had to be away." He paused a moment before saying, "What was Lea like with Amy when she got to Denver? I worried about that."

"She was okay," Karis said. "She loved Amy and I never saw her mistreat or neglect her, even if she wasn't the most attentive or selfless mom. And she did leave Amy with me a lot." So much that Karis had moved to a two-bedroom apartment and set up a permanent nursery for Amy in the second bedroom. But she didn't say that. Instead, she said, "What about you and Lea after Amy was born? How was the marriage then?"

Luke shook his head. "Lea was distant. Withdrawn. Unhappy. Antsy. Bored. Not the person she was when I met her, that was for sure. But she didn't give me any indication that she wanted out. In fact—" Luke breathed a disgusted sort of chuckle "—the day before she bailed she was in a better mood than she had been since Amy's birth, and she said Amy and I were all that mattered to her. Of course twenty-four hours later she was gone and then I knew her improved attitude was because she knew *Abe* was on his way to get her. I guess she was throwing me one last bone."

"But it sounds as if you were happy for a while."

"Happy under false pretenses and then ripped off—I don't think that counts."

"I suppose those hometown girls you'd known all your life looked better to you after that, huh?" Karis tried for even a feeble joke, since he was so ensconced in the negative once again and she wanted to bring him out of it.

Luke's teal eyes were pointedly on her. "I wish that were the case," he said, more to himself than to her. Then he poked his chiseled chin in her direction and said, "What about you? Have you ever been married?"

Maybe her feeble joke had helped after all, she thought, considering it an improvement that he'd changed the subject rather than dwelling on her sister and his past with her.

"No, I've never been married," Karis answered.

"Not even close?"

"Mmm, yeah, I was close. Two times. But neither of them made it."

"Why not?"

"Once was with a guy I'd been seeing for a little over a year. He was in the oil-and-gas business and when his company merged with a company in Texas he was going to have to relocate. He wanted us to get married and move together, but I was worried about leaving Lea and leaving my mom alone to deal with Lea. He wasn't willing to stay in Denver and find another job, so I really looked at it as neither of us being invested enough in the relationship to make it work."

"And the second time?"

"That one was a little more demoralizing. I'd actually accepted Kirk's proposal, because I wanted to marry him. But he didn't meet Lea until after we'd set a date—"

"She stole your fiancé?"

"No, it wasn't like that. But all that free-spirit, fun-loving stuff that got to you, got to Kirk, too, when he finally did meet her. He just…" Karis shrugged. "He wanted her more than he wanted me. Even though she wasn't interested and made that clear. He said that after meeting her, I just didn't seem like enough for him."

"I think you were better off without that guy," Luke said emphatically.

Karis shrugged again. "So no marriages for me."

"But you haven't sworn off the whole idea."

"No. Have you?"

It was nice that he didn't have to think about that for even a moment before he said, "No, I'm sure I'll get married again."

"But you'll run a background check before you do," Karis added, teasing him.

"It's highly likely," he admitted with a laugh.

Karis got up from the table and began to gather the remnants of their snack. Luke stood, too, to help.

"I bow to your sandwich-making expertise," Karis said, once they'd disposed of everything. "But now we need to hit the Halloween candy one more time. Just to keep up tradition."

"What tradition would that be?" he asked.

"The eat-enough-candy-to-induce-sugar-shock-on-Halloween-night tradition. Besides, Amy's too young to eat the stuff and we can't have it going to waste," Karis decreed. "Where did you put it?"

Luke nodded to his left. "Top shelf of the glasses cupboard. I thought it was better to get it out of sight."

"Out of Amy's sight or mine?" Karis asked, going to the cupboard.

"Both," he said, laughing again.

He hadn't only been keeping the plastic pumpkin out of sight, though. It was also out of Karis's reach.

"You're going to make me work for this, aren't you?" she complained, dragging out the small round stool she'd seen in the bottom of the pantry and placing it in the corner of the L formed by the countertop and cupboards.

"It was the only empty spot," he claimed, putting what was left of the sandwich in the refrigerator after wrapping it in plastic as Karis stepped onto the stool.

"Be careful on that thing. It tips," he warned.

No sooner had he said it than the shift of Karis's weight when she reached for the pumpkin caused the stool to veer to one side and slip out from under her just as Luke seemed to dive and half catch her, half shove her onto the countertop to keep her from falling. Getting clunked in the face with the pumpkin in the process.

"Oh! I'm sorry!" Karis said when she had her wits about her again and found herself sitting on the counter with Luke directly in front of her just as one of his hands flew to his eye and the cut brow above it.

"Did I poke your eye out?" she asked in a panic.

"I think you poked it *in*."

Karis dropped the pumpkin onto the counter-top and hopped down to the floor, tugging at Luke's elbow when she got there. "Let me see."

He obliged, but with his injured eye squinted closed.

The cut above it was beginning to bleed, but it was his eye itself she was the most concerned with.

"Can you open it? Can you see?"

He did open it, blinking rapidly and then clamping it shut again.

"I can see. I just need a minute."

"It's probably going to turn black and people will think I beat you up," she lamented.

He laughed.

"Come on, let's get you to the couch," she commanded, leading him by the arm.

"Why do I need the couch?"

"So you can lie down and I can see what kind of damage I did."

"I don't think it's that bad."

Karis ignored the comment and took him into the living room, forcing him to lie flat.

She ran to the bathroom for a Band-Aid and two washcloths, dashed back to the kitchen where she moistened one of them, snatched a bag of frozen peas from the freezer and returned to the living room.

"Frozen peas?" Luke asked when he saw them. "Didn't we just eat?"

"They aren't for eating. They're better than an ice pack because they conform to the wound," she explained as she wrapped the bag of peas in the dry washcloth. "Hold them to your eye while I clean the cut. It isn't bleeding too much, so in a minute we'll put the peas there, too."

"Yes, ma'am," he said, as if accepting orders from a higher-ranking officer, smiling as if he were enjoying himself.

The cut on his head was superficial and once Karis had it cleaned, she said, "I don't think this is deep enough to need stitches. Does your eye feel any better?"

Luke took the peas away, blinked a few times and then left it open. "Seems fine."

Karis took a closer look, trying to ignore how good he smelled when she got that near. "It isn't turning color or swelling yet. Maybe it won't."

"That would be nice since my brother's wedding is tomorrow night. The cut will raise enough questions without a black eye to go with it."

Karis applied the frozen peas to the cut for a few minutes until it had completely stopped seeping blood and then she opened the Band-Aid to cover it.

"Are we done?" Luke asked, still amused by something she was doing—or by something about her—because he kept watching her.

"You tell me. Can you see? Do you have a headache or any dizziness? How do you feel?"

"Like you tried to clean my clock over a few candy bars," he goaded. "But I think I'll live."

Karis remained seated beside him on the couch. She'd been leaning over him, but now she sat straighter. "I said I was sorry," she repeated, less sincerely now that he was obviously all right and merely using the incident to give her a hard time. "That'll teach you not to put chocolate out of my reach. But now that I know I didn't blind you, let's have the candy we nearly sacrificed our lives for."

He laughed. "By all means. We wouldn't want to skip that."

"No, we wouldn't," she confirmed.

She returned to the kitchen to retrieve the pumpkin. When she rejoined him in the living room he was sitting up, his back against the arm of the sofa, his legs still stretched out to take up all but the strip beside him that she'd perched on before.

It was that strip he patted in invitation. "I think I'd better hit the Halloween stash myself after this."

"It does make everything feel better," she agreed. And even though she knew she shouldn't accept the invitation to sit where she'd been sitting before as if she needed to continue ministering to his wounds, she did anyway, holding the pumpkin on her lap.

"What do you want?" she asked.

His smile turned crooked and his gaze was solely on her. "What I shouldn't have," he said, clearly not talking about the candy and sending a warm rush of something very sweet through her bloodstream.

Then he peered down into the pumpkin and said, "I'll take the peanut-butter cup on top."

Karis fished it out and handed it to him, taking a solid chocolate scarecrow for herself.

"Seriously," she said then. "Are you okay?"

He unwrapped his treat and tossed the wrapper onto the coffee table. "I'm fine," he answered and, before he popped the whole thing into his mouth, he added, "What about you? I body-slammed you pretty hard."

Body slam shouldn't have sounded sexy, but it did. At least to Karis, who wasn't particularly eager to let him know that one cheek of her rear end had taken some abuse from the edge of the countertop. She said, "I'm unscathed." At least everywhere that would show. "And the candy is safe," she added, finishing the second half of the scarecrow she'd already taken a bite of.

"I'll bet this was your favorite holiday growing up," he said, when she made it known the chocolate was good.

"I liked the holidays that came with chocolate Santas, chocolate hearts and chocolate bunnies, too. Turkeys and fireworks I could take or leave."

"And what was your favorite costume?" he asked, peering into the pumpkin and choosing a second piece of candy—this one a mint.

Karis's second was a chocolate-covered caramel candy bar that proved to be slightly gooey and required some maneuvering to keep the caramel from dripping. "I didn't have any one favorite costume, but I did like anything with a cape. And I usually kept on wearing the cape until at least Thanksgiving. It gave me flourish." She took a second bite of the caramel bar. "What about you? What was your favorite costume?"

"I was a cop almost every year—not too original, I know."

"But apparently a prediction of your future."

"Apparently," he agreed, grinning again as she finished her candy bar. After a moment, during which he looked as if he were debating something, he reached a thumb to her chin. "Caramel," he explained.

The brush of his thumb only lasted a moment before he took it away, but somehow it set off sparks in Karis. Her own fingertips went to that same spot all on their own, but it had nothing to do with caramel.

"You're sure you can see…and everything?" she asked, telling herself that such a strong reaction to something as simple as wiping her chin was a warning she shouldn't stay where she was.

"I can see…and everything," he answered, his voice slower, more quiet. And since his eyes were intent and piercing all of a sudden, she thought he'd felt the same charge she had. That doubled the reasons she should get away from him, and also kept her there.

Then he raised the same hand he had before, this time to the side of her face, cupping his palm to the line of her jaw and stroking her cheek so softly, so soothingly, that she was lulled even further from thoughts of moving. Especially as his eyes delved into hers and seemed to draw her in.

The hand at her face guided her forward again. Only not to give her a closer look at his cut brow. Instead, he brought her mouth to his.

I shouldn't… I shouldn't… I shouldn't…

But she did. He kissed her and she kissed

him, too, with lips parted and moist from the start. With the same intensity that had been thriving at the end of the second kiss the previous day leaping to life, as if no time had separated that kiss and this one.

Her hand went to his chest and she knew she should use it to push them apart. She knew it. She just couldn't make herself do it. And rather than doing it, her hand drifted up to the side of his neck, holding him to the kiss as surely as he was holding her.

And it all just seemed so normal and natural and familiar. So much as if this was exactly what was meant to be, because it felt absolutely right. It felt so much as if they were in rhythm with each other. Every movement, every nuance. Like long-partnered dancers, no cue was missed, every twist had a turn, every curve had a countercurve, every zig had a zag, as tongues tangoed and took them deeper and deeper into the kiss.

So deep that it began to turn on and tune in the rest of her. The surface of her skin felt all tingly. Her hands, her fingers were ultra aware of each inch of him they explored. Of hair that was soft and bristly at once. Of his beard making a slight reappearance in the hollow of chiseled cheeks and along the sharpness of his own jaw. Of the satiny strength of that unyielding column of neck. Of shoulders broad, straight, steely. Of biceps that were big and round and uncompromising. Of pectorals that were as solid as he was.

Still, they were nothing compared to her own nipples. Nipples that were the only place she was harder than he was. Nipples that had turned to tiny stones as her breasts made themselves and what they wanted known. And what they wanted was to have his hands on them.

His other arm had come around her, had lifted her to sit across his legs, to bring her closer to him. And even though she wasn't near enough for her nipples to have made contact with him, in this, too, she and Luke seemed to be on the same wavelength. Because no sooner had the yearning in Karis arisen than his hand ended its caress of her face to make a descent similar to Karis's own—trailing along the side of her neck to her shoulder, down her arm, to the hem of her sweater where he slipped underneath.

But underneath and around to her back. Low on her back, in the small of it.

She wasn't sure if he was teasing her or waiting to see if she pulled his hand out again before he went any further. But when she found the bottom of his sweater, too, and inched beneath it to the hot silk of his narrow waist, it must have been the permission he was waiting for. Because that was when his hand rose up to the middle of her spine, to where her bra was, and then came forward.

And never before had she wished so fiercely that she'd gone braless! It was just in the way of his hand—that wonderful, adept, agile hand—that she wanted so desperately to feel without anything keeping them apart.

Desperately enough that she reached behind her and unhooked it herself.

Luke chuckled a little even as he kissed her with more abandon, with mouths open wider and tongues carousing.

His free hand came around her hips and pulled her into him, to the ridge waiting to let her know she wasn't the only one of them rife with ideas. Then he eased his hand under her loosened bra to her straining breast.

Karis's breath caught in her throat at that first, fabulous contact of warm hand to soft, engorged flesh. And when her lungs released the air, it came out in a barely audible moan as the man proved he had talents to drive her mad.

Pressing, squeezing, massaging, pulling, tugging—he worked her to a near frenzy that had her nipples so taut she thought they might shatter, until he found those, too. Turning them to crystal pleasures with fingertips that knew just how gentle, just how rough, just how tender and coy and tough to be. And just when to abandon one breast for the other, freeing the first one for the wonders of his mouth when it made that move to new frontiers.

Amazing new frontiers that raised the bar on what he was arousing in her. That had her head falling to one side and her back arching. That had her moaning more audibly and flexing against him without even thinking about the message she was sending this time...

Until he flexed in response.

Until the part of him that was engorged nudged her toward sanity.

Sanity shouting at her that this wasn't only what she shouldn't do.

This was what she *couldn't* do.

Not with this man.

Not with what had come before they'd even known each other.

Not with what she still had to do here.

"Oh, no, Luke, we can't..."

His tongue flicked the very tip of her nipple. Then he stopped, rising to face her as her head fell to his shoulder.

"I'm sorry," she whispered. And she was. Sorrier than she'd ever been in her life to stop something she wanted as much as she wanted him. "I just…this…everything…we should have stayed in the kitchen…."

He laughed a raspy, confused-sounding laugh. "We can move if that's what you want," he offered.

She shook her head. "No. We just can't," she finally said, giving up on trying to be clear.

He nodded, accepting without questioning.

And since she could tell she wasn't helping matters by staying where she was, Karis moved off his lap, sitting again on the edge of the sofa, only this time butted against the side of his thigh rather than angled to face him. Rather than looking at that excruciatingly handsome face or that unbelievable body that she was still starving for.

She shook her head again, dropping it into her hands and letting her hair fall forward like a curtain around her face. "I don't know what there is about us," she whispered.

"Yeah," he agreed.

But she had the impression that he was working too avidly for control to have a conversation so she said, "Maybe I should just go upstairs and give you some time."

"Yeah. Maybe you should. I definitely need a minute."

She stood and had taken several steps towards the entry before his voice stopped her.

"Karis?"

Don't ask me not to go... I won't be able to say no.

"Hmm?" she answered, turning just enough to look at him over her shoulder. To look at the back of his head, because he was facing the other direction.

"Tomorrow night is Reid's wedding. Would you and Amy like to come?"

It was best that he hadn't asked her to rejoin him on the couch, she told herself.

It was also almost unbearably disappointing.

Karis bolstered herself with a deep breath.

"Does your family want us there?" she asked, because while she'd met Reid, his two other brothers had given her a wide berth at the football game.

"I do," Luke said simply. "And my family is all right with whatever I want."

Not a ringing endorsement, but still Karis said, "Okay."

"I need to work part of the day and then do some things at my mother's house to help get ready. But I'll be home to shower and dress, and then we'll go."

"Okay," she repeated.

He didn't say anything else. He merely nodded.

She muttered a good-night and went to the stairs. But she hesitated before going up, pausing to glance at him again, still hoping that he might say something that would take her back to him, still knowing it was best if he didn't.

But there was only silence.

And as she finally climbed the stairs, she wondered if he was listening to her every footfall just as she'd listened to his the night before. If he was thinking what she'd been thinking—about following her. If he was fighting not to.

He didn't follow her, though. And she knew it was a good thing. Because if he had, there wasn't a doubt in her mind that she would have led him to her bedroom. To her bed. To where there would have been no stopping anything.

But this is how it has to be, she told herself.

And she was convinced that was true.

It just didn't keep her from going to the attic wishing that nothing had to be the way it was.

Chapter Eleven

The instant Luke dropped the glass on the bathroom floor he knew he was in trouble. It was a little after three in the morning. The house was dead quiet. And a sonic boom couldn't have sounded louder.

The glass had broken into only three pieces and, sure enough, in the time it took him to pick up those three pieces, Amy was crying.

Much as he would have liked to, it didn't seem fair to wait for her to wake Karis so Karis could put the baby back to sleep, so Luke went into the nursery.

"Shh…it's okay," he said softly to Amy.

The glow of a small night-light was the only illumination in the room and, because he wanted to persuade the baby to lie down and go back to sleep, Luke didn't turn on the overhead light or the small lamp on the bureau. Besides, the night-light was bright enough for him to see that Amy was standing up in the crib, her tiny hands gripping the top rail of the side bars.

It was also bright enough for him to see that she looked terrified, and that her eyes and nose were streaming. When she held out her arms to him, he couldn't very well ignore her. Especially since she'd quieted when she'd first seen him and he knew if he just walked out of the room she'd start crying again.

Reluctantly, he hooked his hands under her arms and lifted her to his hip.

"I couldn't sleep and I was getting a drink of water. I dropped the glass," he explained to her forlorn expression as he grabbed a tissue from the changing table and wiped her nose and dabbed at her cheeks. "I'm sorry I scared you."

"Sca-wuh," she repeated pitifully to confirm that was exactly what he'd done.

"But everything is okay now. Look—" He snatched her elephant from the crib and handed it to her. "You have Eddy to keep you company so you can go back to sleep."

Amy held the toy tight but her bottom lip jutted out and her eyes welled up with fresh tears, letting him know what would come if he tried to simply return her to the crib—elephant or no elephant.

Still, Luke wasn't willing to give up easily. "You can lie down and I'll rub your back," he suggested.

"Sca-wuh," she repeated.

In other words, no deal.

"Okay," he said on a sigh. "How about if I rock you and Eddy for a while and maybe you can go back to sleep that way?"

Amy had no answer. Luke took her silence as consent. And even though it was the last thing he wanted to do, he carried her to the rocking chair anyway and sat down with her in his lap.

That was all it took for her to snuggle her head into his bare chest and put the middle fingers of her free hand in her mouth. But because her eyes stayed wide-open, Luke began to rock.

And to think about something other than Karis for the first time tonight—exactly what he'd been afraid might happen if he ended up like this with Amy.

He'd done pretty much this same thing with her every night for the five weeks he'd believed he was her father. He would come in when she woke for her two-a.m. feeding. He would change her diaper and give her a bottle—things that weren't a necessity now that she ordinarily slept through the night. Then he would take her to this chair and rock her until she dozed off again.

Every night for five weeks it had been just the two of them there in the nursery, in the rocking chair.

And every night he'd sat in awe of how much he'd loved her.

It hadn't mattered if she'd peed on him, pooped on him, or spit up on him. Not a single thing had changed the fact that he'd loved her like nothing and no one ever in his life. Suddenly he'd understood every cliché, every sappy greeting card, everything that had ever been said about what a child could mean to a parent. There wasn't anything he wouldn't have done or given for her—including his own life.

And just remembering it put a lump in his throat.

He'd loved Lea. Or at least he'd thought he had in whatever hormonal infatuation had overcome him. But it hadn't been anything like what he'd felt for Amy. Amy had truly been his heart and soul.

And then Lea had said Amy wasn't his.

He honestly didn't think he could survive that a second time.

Which was why he'd done his damnedest not to get attached to the baby since Karis had brought her here. Why he'd done his damnedest to guard against feeling what he'd felt for her before.

But here he was, sitting in the rocker, with Amy in his lap. Like old times. And it was harder than hell not to recall those other nights like this.

Luke glanced down at Amy to see if she'd fallen asleep yet, hoping she had.

But she hadn't. Her big blue eyes were wide-open, staring up at him.

"Don't look at me like that," he whispered. "I'm just trying to get through this the best way I can."

Amy took her fingers out of her mouth and used the index finger of the same slobbery hand to point to the cut above his eyebrow. "Boo-boo?"

Who could not smile at that?

"Yes, boo-boo."

"Kiss it be-er?"

He laughed. "That's okay. You can kiss it and make it better tomorrow. You just need to go to sleep now."

The fingers returned to her mouth and she wiggled slightly to burrow in closer to him before resting her head against his chest once more.

Luke closed his eyes and clenched his jaw

against the second round of unwanted feelings tonight, not sure which was worse—being so hot for Karis that he'd thought he might burst into flames, or caring for this baby who more than likely wasn't his.

He decided it was a toss-up.

He opened his eyes to look at Amy again and said, "Maybe we should put you back in your bed."

"No," Amy vetoed the idea.

So he didn't do it. He just continued to rock. And tried to keep his feelings in some kind of containment by chanting to himself, *She isn't yours…. She isn't yours…. She isn't yours….*

Nothing—not a single, solitary thing—Lea had done to him was as bad as letting him think Amy was his when she wasn't. Nothing.

And nothing was as difficult for him to do now as keep from hoping that Amy might be his after all.

But he couldn't do it, he told himself. He couldn't. He wouldn't. Because to hope even a little that Amy *was* his was asking for the same kind of pain he'd gone through before when he found out she wasn't. The way he honestly thought he would.

Only he was here in the nursery. In the near-darkness that made time seem almost not to have passed, events seem almost not to have happened. He was here in the rocking chair. And so were the memories…

"I knew just how it would be with you and me," he said quietly. "I was sure I'd be there to see you take your first step, to hear you say your first word. I thought I'd buy you your first bike and teach you how to ride it. I wanted to be the one to take you to school the first day of every year until you made me stop. I figured I'd help you with your math problems and work with you on science projects. I was gonna put your boyfriends through the ringer to make sure they were good enough for you and that they knew better than to mess with you, and I would be waiting up when you got home to flash the porch light on and off so you'd come inside even though it'd probably make you mad. I was planning to take your picture every time you got all dressed up to go to dances, and we were supposed to cut down Christmas trees and decorate them with ornaments we picked out together. I thought I'd be there for every Christmas morning and every birthday and Easter-egg hunt. That I'd teach you to drive a car. And then worry when you did. I hoped you'd stay here for college so I wouldn't have to watch you leave. I even saw myself walking you down the aisle and I knew what I would say to you when I did—"

The lump in his throat had gotten bigger and it momentarily stopped his words.

But when he could he just said, "Yeah, I had some plans," rather than torturing himself remembering any more of what those plans had been.

He glanced down at Amy and discovered that he'd talked her to sleep. And while he'd thought that was the answer to his problems, the sight of her there, cuddled to his chest, her long lashes resting on her chubby cheeks, cracked the wall he thought he'd erected around his heart when it came to her. And he was suddenly flooded with so many of the feelings he'd had for her during those five weeks that it was as if he'd been hit with a battering ram.

He clamped his eyes shut again, fighting everything—the emotions, the images of Amy at that moment, the images of them both at different intervals in the future, the horrible hope he didn't want to have.

She isn't mine…. She isn't mine…. She isn't mine….

He took a breath, held it until his lungs hurt enough to demand air and the physical pain forced him to focus on that rather than on anything else he felt. Then he exhaled and stood.

He returned Amy to her crib, relieved that she remained asleep as he laid her down—elephant and all—and covered her.

But still there was another moment when he couldn't make himself move from beside her crib. When he stood there watching her sleep.

When, for just that one moment, he couldn't help wondering *what if.*

What if she *was* his.

On the surface, as Karis attended the wedding of Luke's brother Reid and Chloe Carmichael Wednesday evening, Karis fit in just fine.

The advantage of having everything she owned in her car rather than having merely packed a suitcase to come to Northbridge was that, when it came to dressing up, she'd had something she could wear.

She'd merely had to have Luke open the trunk of her car, where she'd located the dress she'd worn to the wedding of a co-worker on Labor Day weekend.

It was a navy-blue number that, while it was only one piece, appeared to be a short strapless dress underneath a lace overlay that provided a ballet neckline and long sleeves. The dress was formfitting and short, and she also still had the navy-hued thigh-high nylons she'd worn and the two-inch-high sling-back shoes that were nothing but soles held onto her feet by thin, crisscross straps.

She'd left her hair loose for the occasion, and allowed the natural curl she usually eased out of it with a large-barreled curling iron to flourish by scrunching it while it dried after her shampoo. Then she'd applied a hint of taupe eye shadow, more mascara than usual, a bit darker blush, and she'd used lipstick rather than gloss to complete the effect that had won her the interest of no fewer than four men at the Labor Day wedding.

Because that event had occurred just before Lea's last debacle, Lea had still been working with Karis, and so both Lea and Amy had also gone to the wedding. Which meant that Amy had her own frilly pink dress and black patent-leather shoes to wear, too.

The Walker wedding itself couldn't have been more lovely. It was a small, cozy affair of bride, groom, three bridesmaids and three groomsmen. The guests numbered less than fifty in the living room of the family home.

Candles lit the proceedings and the air was filled with the scent of autumn-toned wildflowers—yellow, gold, rust and orange blossoms with a few deep purple buds interspersed for contrast.

The bride wore a mid-calf-length gown of creamy satin that was empire-waisted and strapless. The groom and his groomsmen brothers all wore dress suits the dark brown of espresso with café au lait shirts, and ties that picked up the colors of both suit and flowers.

After the brief ceremony, which was solemn, joyous and humorous all at once, the dinner and reception that followed were nothing so much as a house party. A house party where everyone knew and liked everyone else and threw themselves into the celebration of the marriage of two people who had been in love long ago, torn apart, only to rediscover each other years later.

The whole thing was wonderful to watch and made Karis terribly sad.

She was treated well. Walkers and Pratts and everyone else were all pleasant to her. There wasn't a conversation or a toast or anything else that she wasn't included in. She just knew—and couldn't forget—that in a way she was on probation for what Lea had done here. That despite the appearance that she was a part of things, she wasn't.

And she discovered that while before, when she'd appreciated the close family atmosphere of the entire community and enjoyed being included in things with her half siblings, now she just desperately wanted to genuinely belong to what she saw around her. To be one of them. Really, truly one of them.

And she knew she couldn't be.

She tried to take comfort in the fact that if she left Amy behind, Amy would be embraced and let into the inner circle that was Northbridge. She tried to be grateful for that as she watched everyone dote on the adorable baby.

But the thought of not having her niece with her only made the sadness worse and for herself, more than at any other time since she'd arrived in the small town, Karis felt she was pressing her nose against the window of a chocolate factory she had no hope of getting into. No matter how hungry she was for what was inside. And she *was* hungry for it. Starved for it. Especially when she thought that when she left here she would be going someplace where she had no family at all if she didn't have Amy.

It *was* good for Amy, though, Karis kept telling herself.

And that was important.

It just didn't make her feel any better.

It was almost eleven that night when there was a knock on the door of the attic bedroom.

Karis, Luke and Amy had left the wedding reception shortly after ten o'clock. Karis had taken the overly tired baby out of her party clothes, put her in her sleeper and watched her fall asleep the moment her head hit the crib pillow. Then Karis had gone to her own room, where she'd just kicked off her shoes and removed her nylons when the knock sounded.

"Yeah?" she called, knowing it had to be Luke on the other side of the door.

"Are you decent?"

"Sure."

"Can I come in?"

She had no idea why he wanted to. This evening hadn't been like the last three, when talking had brought them closer and they'd ended up kissing. And more. When she'd considered following him to his bedroom and wondered if he might follow her to hers.

Tonight they'd been with so many other people that they'd only been alone during the five-minute drives to and from his family's house. So everything between them had been friendly and cordial and not at all intimate— exactly as it should have been. Even if it had only added to the melancholy she'd felt throughout the evening.

But at least she knew he wasn't coming to her

room for any forbidden reason, so she said, "Sure, come in."

He opened the attic door and stepped inside.

The suit coat and tie that had made him seem distinguished were gone, but he still looked wonderful in the slacks and the shirt that now had the top two buttons undone.

"What's up?" Karis asked when he made it a few feet into the room, his hands in his trouser pockets, his weight slung more on one hip than the other.

"I don't know. You tell me. You weren't yourself tonight."

"Who was I?" she joked without much oomph because she didn't have any to put into it.

"I don't know. You were quiet. You kind of stood back—"

"Am I usually loud and dancing on tabletops?"

"No, but…I don't know. I know we were in a rush getting to the wedding, so I didn't even get the chance to tell you how great you looked, which, by the way, you did. That dress is a knockout."

"Thank you," she said, feeling only slightly better when the compliment came out with awe attached to it.

"But you didn't say much to me or to anyone else the whole night. You just sort of stayed on the sidelines. And Amy talked on the way home."

"Because she wanted a third slice of wedding cake and couldn't understand that even though we were taking some home for her she couldn't have it right then."

Luke nodded and didn't say anything else for a moment, merely standing there, staring at her as if those beautiful teal-green eyes of his were trying to read what was wrong with her in the way she looked.

When Karis didn't offer more, he said, "You're doing a lot of dancing around what I'm asking and not answering any of it. Did the teasing about my eye get to you?"

There was a purplish crescent moon under the eye she'd hit with the pumpkin and a slight swelling to his brow today. Neither of them detracted from how traffic-stoppingly handsome he was, but they were enough to inspire questions and the ensuing jokes about how she'd beaten him up.

"No, I didn't mind that," she assured him, because it was true. It had all been good-natured.

"Then what's going on, Karis? Because something is. I can see it."

She didn't want to tell him. It seemed so pathetic and self-pitying. But she also didn't want her contemplative mood to raise his suspicions again and she decided the only way to prevent that was to be honest with him.

She sat on the side of the brass bed's mattress and shrugged. "It's just really nice here," she said, trying to keep her tone more casual than morose.

"Here?"

"In Northbridge. It actually *is* the way small towns are supposed to be, and I guess I was soaking it in."

"It didn't seem like you were *enjoying* soaking it in."

"I was, though. I had a good time tonight."

"It didn't seem like that, either," he persisted, coming to stand with one hand on the brass foot rail.

He studied her once more. Then he reached out and took her hand, surprising her. "I haven't thought about it before, but when you leave here you don't have much of anything—or anyone— waiting for you anywhere else, do you?" he said, squeezing her hand comfortingly.

"Nope," she said, trying to sound glib. And failing.

"All you have left is Amy. Or do you have family on your mother's side?"

"Not anymore."

"So there's only you and Amy, and you

brought Amy here. And tonight you were with all of my family—and there's getting to be a lot of it. And you were with the other Pratts, who are warming to you, I think, but who aren't treating you like family. And you felt like an outsider and it made you think about losing the family you *did* have. And you were miserable."

"Not miserable," she amended. "But yes, a lot of that went through my mind. And I guess that made tonight good *and* bad."

"I'm sorry," he said as if, for the first time since they'd met, he'd actually put aside his own feelings where Lea was concerned and was only thinking of Karis. From Karis's perspective. "Probably not even chocolate will help out with this one, will it?" he added with a sympathetic smile.

"It doesn't sound good, no," Karis said with a small smile of her own.

"So what should I do with you?" he said, looking at the hand he held, smoothing the back of it with his thumb.

"You don't have to do anything with me. I'm fine."

"I could fill the tub with bubbles and you could soak away your troubles."

It flashed through her mind that that only had appeal if he got into it with her. But of course she couldn't say that, so she said, "The rhyme was good but that's okay."

"I could make you a cup of tea—my mother drinks chamomile when she's blue. And puts a heavy shot of bourbon in it—she always feels better after that."

Karis laughed. "I'll bet she does."

"How about it, then? Spiked tea, I could make a fire again. We can sit in front of it and you can be as maudlin as you want. You can even cry and carry on."

She laughed again. "Ooo, that sounds like fun," she said facetiously. "Especially for you."

"I'll tough it out," he offered.

"No. Thanks anyway."

"Would you like to bay at the moon? Because we can get out onto the roof from up here and you can caterwaul till your heart's content."

"Caterwaul? What is caterwaul?"

"It's a lot like crying and carrying on only louder and more public."

"Ah, that would give your neighbors something to talk about."

"Or you could throw things—baseballs tossed at metal trash cans make a lot of noise. It's cathartic."

"Is that what you do to work out your bad moods?"

"As a kid it was."

"I think I'll pass," she said.

"What am I going to do then? I can't just leave you up here alone to suffer."

"I'm not *suffering*," she insisted. "Besides, you've already made me feel better." And he had just by making light of it all.

He wiggled his uninjured eyebrow at her. "How did I do that?"

"By being a goofball."

"I beg your pardon. I'm being so damn sensitive I could get an award and you're calling me a goofball?"

That really made her laugh. "You *are* being so damn sensitive you could get an award," she agreed.

"So what do I get?" he asked.

She almost said *me,* because that was what flashed through her mind, the way the idea of him joining her in a bubble bath had. He could be so disarming. And so charming and sweet and sexy. And she was feeling even more vulnerable than she had any of the evenings before.

Which she knew had her treading a very fine line.

So in answer to his question about what kind of an award he deserved, she stood and used the hand he was holding to lead him toward her door.

"You get to relax and go to bed without thinking I'm in some kind of funk that you need to get me out of."

"Huh, that doesn't sound like much fun, either," he muttered.

"More fun than caterwauling or baying at the moon or crying and carrying on."

He went through the doorway when they arrived there, but he still didn't let go of her hand, keeping hold of it when he turned to face her.

His expression was serious again but not solemn or sober, just sincere as he looked down at her. "You're sure you're okay?" he asked as if he genuinely cared.

"I'm sure."

He gently conformed his free hand to her cheek. "Because I don't want you feeling bad."

What she was feeling was warm honey sluicing from his palm all through her veins.

"I don't feel bad," she assured, but somehow her voice had gone quiet. And alluring. Even though that was completely unintentional.

"But you don't feel like company?" he asked.

His own tone was different suddenly, too. Insinuating. In response to hers, maybe. And despite the fact that Karis knew it shouldn't be the case, she was regretting that she'd shown him her door and given the impression that she didn't want his company. Because with each passing moment, she wanted it more and more. But not in the way he'd offered it before.

She didn't answer his question. Instead she merely looked up into his eyes.

And that was when her vulnerability to him won out. That was when the loneliness that had been dogging her all evening made saying good-night to him and staying alone in her room the last thing she could make herself do. That was when looking up into the face that haunted her dreams, at the man who had an inexplicable pull on her, became all that mattered.

That was when she knew that after everything she'd been through because of other people and for other people, she'd finally reached a time that had to be only for her. A time when just one thing was important—vital—to her. And that one thing was Luke. Luke and just a brief while of not saying no to her own urges, her own inclinations or desires. Without thinking about anything but the two of them. Without anything else intruding.

And without worrying whether or not she should.

"If I said I do want company, would you stay just because you feel sorry for me?"

He gave her a lopsided, sheepish grin. "Okay,

so maybe I'm not *that* sensitive. The way you look in that dress drove me wild all night. I don't want you to be sad and I really did want to cheer you up, but cheering you up just gave me an excuse to be with you again tonight."

"There were ulterior motives behind your sensitivity?" she joked, hiding that she was glad to hear it, to know that he had had the same designs on her that she had on him.

"I wouldn't say it was that calculated. Especially not when I've been trying to talk myself out of any more nights like last night. I'm just saying that if you want me to stay, no, I wouldn't be with you because I feel sorry for you."

"And what about talking yourself out of any more nights like last night? You must have reasons—"

But whatever those reasons were, they were apparently taking a back seat tonight the same way hers were, because before she could complete what she'd been about to say, he leaned in and kissed her. With lips parted when they met hers. With the hand he was holding brought up to his chest. With his tongue not waiting for an invitation before jutting in and out to let her know what he had on his mind.

Then he stopped kissing her and, in a voice already smoky with arousal, he said, "I have plenty of reasons for not doing this. But tonight I just don't care what they are. All I care about is that I want you so much it's killing me."

He turned then, taking her with him away from the attic room.

"Where are we going?" she asked.

"Where I'm better equipped."

"Equipped?"

He cast her a wicked grin as they went down the stairs to the second floor and into his bedroom.

The only light was coming from outside—moonglow mostly—but it was enough for her to see his king-size bed made up in a dark gray down comforter and the condoms he took out of the nightstand drawer beside it.

"Equipment," he said, showing them to her before leaving them on the top of the nightstand.

"I was afraid it might be handcuffs," she joked again.

"Uh-uh. I only want you willingly," he said as his attention returned to her.

He let go of her hand then, cupping both sides of her face to kiss her again. And again there was nothing in the kiss but raw desire to match what was spurring her on.

Karis placed her hands on his chest and made one final decision to suspend everything else for tonight and just give in to what had been happening between them almost from the start.

He combed his fingers through her hair to pull her more firmly into the kiss as mouths opened and tongues played games they'd invented in nights gone by, unrestrained, rash and reckless.

For Karis there was such release and exhilaration in ending the battle to ignore her yearnings for this man that she gave as good as she got, playing uninhibitedly even as she succumbed to one more inclination the moment it struck her. She unfastened the buttons of his shirt and pressed her palms to his bare chest in order to absorb the feel of flesh over the wall of his muscles.

Hot, smooth skin encasing honed pectorals and taut male nibs that tensed even more when she touched them, toyed with them, teased them a little. Then she let her hands follow his sides downward to pull his shirttails totally free.

Mouths were opened wide and he was kissing her so fiercely that her head was tipped far back, putting her hair in the way of his finding the top of the dress's zipper. He managed, though, and once he had, he guided the zipper's pull to its bottommost point and then slipped his hands inside the lace to her shoulders. Strong hands that massaged away any remnants of tension and made her whole body crave their touch.

The dress had a built-in bra, so when he eased it off and let it fall around her feet, she was left in nothing but panties. The room wasn't particularly chilly, but still the sudden exposure sent a shiver through her that he felt.

He wrapped her in his arms and pulled her close against him where the heat of his chest met her breasts. Still her nipples stayed diamond-hard because cold wasn't the cause for their standing alert.

Karis took off his shirt, wanting nothing to interfere with the meeting of his flesh and hers. And once his shirt had joined her dress on the floor, she moved on, insinuating her hands between them to unhook the waistband of his suit pants as mouths continued their hungry plundering.

Even her formfitting dress had been shed easier than his pants because of the burgeoning proof that he wanted her as much as she wanted him. But with some finesse they went down, too, leaving him in boxers that barely contained him.

His exposure didn't make him shiver the way

hers had. But it did kick things up a notch. Luke lowered her to the bed, taking off her panties the moment she was lying down and sending what remained of his own things flying as well. Then he lay beside her, his astonishing body partially on top of her as his hand found the straining mound of her breast.

There wasn't anything she needed more right then, and she couldn't help swelling into his palm in an undulation that mimicked an ocean wave.

His mouth deserted hers to nibble her ear, to send the tip of his tongue inside it to a spot she hadn't known existed. A special spot that somehow turned up the heat in her a dozen degrees more.

Between the stroke of that tongue and a hand that worked miracles at her breast—kneading, caressing, massaging, tugging and teasing and circling her nipple—she couldn't keep her breath from catching in her lungs, her spine from curling away from the mattress, her body from writhing.

Her own hands went on a quest of their own, finding him all sleek, lean and oh so well muscled. She traveled the breadth of his shoulders and trailed down his back to the derriere that felt every bit as perfect as it looked. She straightened her elbows to course down thick thighs and then she drew forward and came up, touching the part of him that could make him moan.

Long and thick and gloriously rigid, she stroked him, too, doing her own part to build the intensity and raise the bar.

His mouth found her breast, taking it fully into the hot, damp darkness where his tongue flicked the tip of her nipple. Where his teeth tenderly tugged. Where everything he was doing tightened something that ran like a core through the center of her, from there downward, awakening so much more.

His free hand glided smoothly from just beneath the swell of her breast along her rib cage to her stomach and beyond, showing no shyness in finding that most secluded spot and sliding inside her. Inside and then out. Once. Twice. Three times. Until her back again came away from the mattress as her own need for even more reached a new level.

Her legs opened and one went over his hip even as she echoed his earlier moan.

He took his hand away from her and hers away from him then, rolling away briefly to use his *equipment* before rising above her to position himself just so. To find the same portal his fingers had tantalized with that bigger and better part of his body, slipping into her in one even, effortless, fluid motion.

And then there he was, his hands on either side of her head, his strong arms holding his upper half above her while their lower halves fused.

He dipped down to kiss her again—the sexiest, most erotic kiss anyone had ever given her—and then he began to move.

His fingers had only been a sneak preview. A teaser for the full feature.

Painstakingly slow. Careful. Measured. In and out. Each thrust raising the anticipation, the need for the next.

A little faster. Just enough.

A little deeper. Just enough.

Faster still.

Deeper still.

He came into her and she rose to meet him. She tightened around him. He retreated and so did she. Only to return. For more. For more. For more. Until his pace was so quick, so vigorous, so turbulent, she could only hang on for the wild, tumultuous ride.

Closer and closer she went toward losing herself in all he was bringing to life within her, all he was arousing within her, setting loose within her. Gaining. Growing. Flourishing and expanding until it catapulted her to a peak so indefinably incredible that it was as if even her heartbeat stood still for that one blindingly profound moment when everything burst into excruciating bliss.

And then there was only the free fall back into reality. Into the reality where Luke's magnificent body took one last plunge into the depths of her before he tensed and froze in ecstasy of his own, catching Karis and taking her with him a second time that didn't match the first but still left her wilted with divine satiety as he relaxed—muscle by muscle, inch by inch—to lie only then with all of his weight on her.

His breath was steamy in her hair. Hers ricocheted against his shoulder. The same shoulder she kissed a moment later when she began to function again.

He bowed his head to hers and kissed her, too, before she felt him smile.

"I don't know what to say except wow!" he whispered in a gravelly whisper.

Karis laughed weakly. "Me, too."

He maneuvered his arms around her and took her with him to lie on their sides, their bodies still one, his right leg over her hip.

Her face was close to his chest, and his big body cocooned hers. It was as if he were her whole universe right there and then. And she felt safe, exhausted, wonderful.

"Let's get some sleep and do it all over again," he said, after placing another kiss on the crown of her head.

"Okay," she agreed, half-thinking he was kidding.

"You won't go anywhere?"

She shook her head.

He settled then and so did she, too weary to do more than close her eyes and yield to fatigue. Too content to think about anything that might make this any less perfect than it was.

This single, flawless here-and-now that she'd allowed herself before she had to go on with what she needed to do.

Chapter Twelve

The second day of November dawned cold, bright and sunny. Luke saw it firsthand, hunched inside his heaviest winter coat, a cup of steaming coffee in his gloved grip, standing in the woods.

He'd been sound asleep in his warm bed after a night of more romping than resting, with Karis in his arms, their naked limbs entwined, when the phone had jolted him awake before sunrise. And despite the fact that he was supposed to have Thursday off, after answering that call, he'd had no choice but to press a kiss to Karis's forehead, advise her to go back to sleep, and slip

out of bed to dress and meet his fellow Northbridge police officers approximately fifty yards
southwest of the old north bridge.

Where human skeletal remains had been
located.

Cutty Grant and the fourth member of Northbridge's police force were closer to the site
while Cam and Luke took up the rear, behind
the state search team, more state cops and a
contingent of FBI agents who all watched a forensics unit work the site itself.

"Apparently the search team found the grave
late yesterday and opted to call their own guys
and the feds before letting us know. We weren't
notified until everyone else was already arriving
this morning," Cam told Luke, speaking softly
enough so only he could hear.

"Jerks," Luke said, not appreciating the dis-
respect shown toward the local force but also
not unhappy that he'd been left in the dark long
enough to attend his brother's wedding and
have the night he'd had with Karis. In fact, he
would have been happy if he hadn't been called
in for a couple more hours, because he'd had
plans for how he was going to wake Karis up
this morning and those plans hadn't involved
him abandoning her in bed.

But he couldn't think about that right then,

when day off or no day off, he had to focus on work and what one of the forensics team members had apparently faced the group at large to announce.

"What we have here," the man began, "are the remains of a full-grown male who, at first inspection, appears to have died from a blow to the head. Although there isn't any identification, based on the decomposition, on the dated clothes and shoes, and on a ring we've found with the initials MR, this looks to be your missing bank robber, Mickey Rider."

"You know what this means, don't you?" Cam said in an aside to Luke as other officials talked amongst themselves.

"That since the state guys know both robbers are dead and that there's no indication that Celeste Perry is, they'll probably consider her a prime suspect in a murder case and we're going to be looking hard for her now," Luke responded.

"You got it," Cam confirmed.

"The Reverend isn't going to be pleased," Luke concluded.

"And we'd better do some real work coming up with how Celeste's appearance might have changed," Cam added. "That old picture of her hasn't done us any good yet. It definitely isn't going to cut it from here on."

"We may be in luck on that front," Luke said. "Faith Perry just told me last night at the wedding that her sister Eden is moving back to town."

"No," Cam countered, as if that thought didn't sit well with him.

"According to Faith, she is," Luke confirmed. "And you know Eden is a forensic artist. Maybe we could get her to do an age progression and a weight-increased image to give us a better idea how Celeste's appearance might have changed, so we can get a handle on whether or not she passed through here again after she left that night. Or even stuck around by some chance if she did get back—the way you said."

"But Eden Perry…" Cam complained.

Luke knew his confusion had to show. "You have a problem with Eden Perry?"

Cam shrugged but offered no information.

Luke went on. "Anyway, Faith said she was coming back to Northbridge because she's getting out of that line of work, but maybe we can persuade her to do one last job."

"Maybe you or somebody else can. But count me out. She was never my favorite person," Cam said, his tone dour enough to make that sound like an understatement.

"Favorite person or not, she still seems like our best bet for the next step," Luke persisted in spite of his friend's obvious and unexplained distaste for Eden Perry.

Cam just scowled and walked away as if he wanted a closer look at the grave site.

And Luke was left more curious about his friend's reaction than about the just-unearthed skeleton.

As far as he knew, the last time Cam and Eden Perry had had any contact at all was in high school, where Eden had been one of those people who blended into the wallpaper, while Cam had been a Northbridge superstar.

Given that dynamic, Luke would have guessed that Cam wouldn't have had reason to take much notice of Eden, let alone be carrying around so much distaste for her all these years later.

"Huh," Luke said to himself. "I wonder what's up with that."

But he figured only time would tell, since clearly Cam wasn't talking.

It was nine in the morning when Luke returned home. He'd known it was a long shot to hope that Amy might still be asleep. That he might find Karis still in bed, too. That he might be able to slip in beside her and initiate the day the way he'd wanted to before the predawn phone call had taken him away.

But one glance through the living room's picture window told him that long shot hadn't paid off.

He could see through to the kitchen from there and Amy was in the high chair with Karis sitting facing her, feeding her breakfast, both of them in profile.

Luke took a resigned, disappointed breath and sighed. And then discovered that even though he might not be able to go in and hop back into bed with Karis, he was just as eager to get inside to what *was* going on.

Amy was still in her sleeper, her curly hair tousled, her toy elephant stuffed into the high chair beside her. Her little mouth kept opening for each spoonful of oatmeal as it was offered and she looked almost unfathomably cute and cuddly and endearing.

And there was Karis.

She must have stayed awake after he'd left, because she was dressed in jeans and a red mock-turtleneck sweater that buttoned up the front. Her flawless face was bright and cheery and beautiful. Each time she turned her head to take something from the table, he could see her eyes, big, round, lake-blue eyes that were more defined when she fixed herself up for the day. Plus her auburn hair was shiny clean and rather than being tied in the ponytail she put it in before washing it in the morning, it was hanging free and smooth and turned under on the ends.

Luke could just imagine what she smelled like, too. Fresh from her shower. All clean and sweet and flowery.

She was talking to Amy as she fed her. Smiling at the baby. Making the meal fun. Pretending to eat whatever Amy refused so it would seem more enticing. Sneaking a bite of jellied toast here and there for herself.

Despite the fact that he'd hoped to start this day more amorously, what he was finding now was a nice consolation. And all of a sudden the sense that he was coming home to his family hit him.

Just before he recalled that this *wasn't* his family. At least as far as he knew.

The impact deflated him. Instead of going inside, he leaned against the porch railing, continuing to stare through the window at the picture-perfect tableau before him, knowing he had to sort through whatever was going on with him before he did any more playing at family man.

Then it occurred to him that he didn't really want to stop playing family man.

She's Lea's sister, he told himself, trying to more firmly fix the connection in his brain.

Because along the way, he seemed to have lost sight of it.

Karis and Lea—same genes, raised in the same environment, by the same people.

But something in him balked at the thought he'd had when he'd first met Karis. Especially as he went on watching her.

Karis and Lea *weren't* the same people.

There was evidence of that right in front of him. In the loving care Karis showed Amy.

Amy came first with Karis. Karis was endlessly patient with her. Interested in her. Delighted by her. Wanting only her well-being and what was best for her.

No matter what Karis said about her sister and her sister as a mother, Luke had seen what kind of mother Lea was. It was nothing like the kind of mother Karis was to Amy. Without even being Amy's mother.

There just wasn't anything else about Karis that was like Lea, either, he thought, struggling to come up with something that made them similar. But nothing he'd seen from her had made him think of Lea.

That was part of what had gotten him to this point, he realized. Because if Karis *had* reminded him of Lea, it would have been a huge turnoff. And he was anything but turned off by Karis.

Continuing to stand there in the cold, he recalled something he'd said about her, something he'd guessed when she'd told him about her growing-up years, about how she'd tried to comfort her mother when her father had abandoned them and when her mother had had to deal with problems with Lea. She'd said that she'd become the good girl to balance the trouble Lea had caused and he'd christened her the responsible one.

She'd made light of that, but Luke really thought about it now and decided he'd been right.

Again, in Karis's care of Amy, there was certainly responsibility. But there were also indications of it in the lengths she was going to to repay her former employers the money Lea had stolen. There was proof of her being a responsible, conscientious person in everything the Denver cops had said about her both times he'd called to verify her stories—stories that had checked out.

There were even signs of her sense of responsibility in her reluctance to take anything from him without making the deal to work for her keep. A deal she'd honored by cleaning his house. By preparing meals and doing laundry. By fixing nail holes and wall marks and carpet stains that the renters had left behind.

That was definitely nothing like Lea. Responsible was not something anyone could ever say she'd been.

There was also support for Karis not being like Lea in the fact that he'd left a little money out here and there—not a lot, just some pocket change and petty cash in case something came up while he was at work. But Karis hadn't touched a cent of it, while it would have disappeared ten times over with Lea around.

No, he had to admit that Karis wasn't Lea. She wasn't like Lea.

And if he considered Karis on her own merits?

She was kind, considerate, compassionate, good-natured, agreeable, not greedy or demanding. She found joy and pleasure in small things— like Northbridge's Halloween. She was funny and sharp and smart. Beautiful and so sexy she made his blood run faster just thinking about her.

He could go on and on about the merits of Karis. What he couldn't do was come up with any *demerits*.

But then maybe that was because he liked her. So damn much.

So damn much that he wanted to be with her every minute. He thought about her nonstop. He dreamed about her. He considered what she might like or dislike, what might or might not please her, thrill her, make her laugh. It had given him a warm rush to look across the room during Reid's wedding and see her. To know she was with him. That at the end of the evening he would get to bring her home with him, that that wouldn't be the end of his time with her. That she'd be there when he went to bed and still be there when he woke up. That she'd be there when he got off work or came home from anything else—just as he was now. And that had made him feel good. Great. Terrific.

Everything about her, every minute he spent with her, made him feel terrific.

With his gaze still trained on the two females in his life, he watched Amy refuse the same bite of cereal for the third time. That meant she wasn't likely to accept it, but still Karis tried a fourth time and Amy showed the stubbornness she could trot out now and then.

It could be frustrating and while Karis handled it with aplomb, it turned Luke's thoughts to the baby.

Amy.

His or not his?

If she *was* his, then she *was* his family. His responsibility. His future. And for the first time he let down all his guards and acknowledged that he hoped it was true. That he actually hoped Amy was his. Because even though intellectually he doubted that she was, deep down she *felt* like his.

But what if she *wasn't* his? he asked himself, thinking still about Karis.

Because even if Amy *wasn't* his, any relationship with Karis—if that was what he was standing on the porch considering—would include Amy. So what if he acted on what he was feeling about Karis, and the DNA test proved Amy had been fathered by someone else?

He waited for the internal, protective recoil the thought had caused him since Lea had said it. But this time it didn't happen.

Because as he studied the baby he could see clearly what he'd thought when Karis had initially shown up—that Amy really was a clean slate. Regardless of who her biological father was, she was an innocent. Innocent of anything and everything that had come before her. And whether or not she did carry his genetic material, whether or not he tried to keep her at a distance, whether or not he fought it, the truth was that he'd fallen in love with the little girl the day she was born and that love for her was still there. When all was said and done, when the resentments of her mother were stripped away, waiting underneath his own bruised ego and pride, he still loved Amy. She was the child of his heart no matter what.

The child of his heart being cared for by the woman who had—almost overnight—become the woman of his heart, too.

Almost overnight.

It was all happening so fast.

Again.

Not quite as fast as things had happened with Lea, but close. And *that* was something he'd sworn never to do again. That was something that made him very nervous.

Very, very nervous.

And yet, despite the nervousness, and try though he did, he couldn't convince himself that there was anything wrong with what he was feeling about Karis. About Amy. He couldn't convince himself there was anything wrong with either of them or with wanting the family that wasn't his family to *be* his family.

He rolled that around in his mind for a while, looking at it from every angle. Trying it on like a new pair of shoes to see if it really did fit. He wondered if he'd gone insane a second time in less than two years. He even imagined what he would say to his family, to his friends, who would undoubtedly think he *had* lost his mind again.

But none of it had the kick to it that was there, in front of his face, as he watched Karis wipe Amy's mouth and kiss her forehead. As he watched Amy pucker up to offer a kiss in return and Karis laughingly accept it.

Because at that moment he knew without question that regardless of the past, of genetics, of family ties, regardless of how quickly this had come to be for him or of how it might be viewed by anyone else, he wanted his part of what was going on inside. He wanted to be with Karis and Amy as a family. He wanted to be a father to Amy whether he technically was or not.

And he wanted Karis just because she was Karis.

He wanted Karis in his kitchen as she was now. In his living room fussing over him as she had Halloween night or sitting in front of the fire with him as she had Sunday night. He sure as hell wanted Karis in his bedroom. In his bed.

He wanted Karis in his life for all the time to come and without any of the past dragging behind them.

Of course that would be easier said than done since she was still in debt to her former employers.

But she could pay that off faster if she was there with him and then they honestly could be free of the past. Of Lea and all Lea had wrought.

He thought they both deserved that. They'd both earned it.

And with his decision made, he finally headed for the front door.

Not entertaining a single thought that there might be any more complications than those he'd already hashed through.

"You look so cold! Let me get you a cup of coffee," Karis said, when she glanced up from cleaning Amy's breakfast mess and saw Luke standing in the entry to the kitchen.

His cheeks and nose were apple-red with chill and it made her shiver to look at him. There was also an element of tension that went with the shiver, because, in the light of day, the way they'd spent the previous night was worrying her considerably. Along with the uncertainty of where they would go from here.

But at that moment she put her worries aside and concentrated on the more immediate matters at hand.

"No, thanks. I've had three cups of coffee already this morning," Luke said. "But I do want to talk to you."

That sounded weighty and Karis assumed the same things that were troubling her were on his mind, too. So she said, "I know. We definitely need to talk." But she was shy about looking at him so she finished washing off the high-chair tray.

As she did she couldn't help watching him out of the corner of her eye, though. He left the doorway and came to stand behind the high chair, bending over and kissing the top of Amy's head.

"Good morning, sweet girl."

Karis's eyebrows flew up at his actions. Luke had never greeted Amy so demonstrably before. Why was he now?

"Dow?" Amy responded to the greeting, wanting out of the high chair.

"I'll get you down in a minute," Karis said.

Luke stepped around the high chair and took off his gloves, stuffing them into the pocket of the fleece-lined suede coat he had on with the collar turned up around his also-red ears. He unbuttoned the coat and took it off, slinging it over the back of one of the kitchen chairs.

"Nothing's wrong, is it?" he asked, apparently noticing the nervousness in Karis's jerky motions as she ended up wiping more toast crumbs onto the floor than into her hand. "Because what I want to talk about is that I think things are actually pretty right," he added.

Wondering what that meant, Karis paused to look at him.

He gave her a sexy, intimate smile that she couldn't help answering with a small smile of her own despite her concerns.

"Last night," she guessed, thinking that was what he wanted to talk about.

"Last night was amazing," he said as if he were agreeing with her.

So amazing that just the memory of it made Karis feel warm all over.

"But last night only got me started thinking this morning," Luke continued. "Seeing you and Amy through the front window when I got home just now and what it did to me is what I want to talk about."

Karis had no idea what he meant as she took in the sight of him in jeans and a heavy brown tweed henley sweater that added bulk to his astounding shoulders, pectorals and biceps. But she tried not to focus on how much she wanted to take off the sweater and have free reign over what was beneath it, knowing that they really *did* need to talk and that since he'd started it, now was the time.

Luke took the sponge from her and tossed it into the sink. Then he reached for her hand.

"Sit down," he urged, spinning the chair she'd been sitting in to feed Amy so that it faced another chair.

"Dow!" Amy repeated more insistently.

Luke left Karis to sit and went to the cupboard, getting graham crackers to bring back to the table with him. Amy adored graham crackers and was easily occupied with the one Luke gave her before sitting in the chair across from Karis and scooting forward until her knees were between his spread thighs. Then he took both of her hands in his.

It didn't matter that his were still cool from his stay outside. His touch sent sparkles up her arms and all through her. Karis was confused, however, because this didn't seem like a setup for the kind of conversation she'd been thinking they needed to have. So she merely waited for him to begin.

When he did, he began where he'd left off. "I was coming home, hoping Amy would still be sleeping and you'd be in bed, too, so I could crawl back in with you."

Karis felt her cheeks heat, less from embarrassment than from what flashed through her mind at the thought of what would have happened had he rejoined her in bed and how much she wished it had.

"But then I saw you," he went on. "And after some disappointment, it dawned on me that coming home to this was good, too. It felt like coming home to my family."

Still confused as to what he was getting at, Karis said, "Amy may be your family."

"She may be. But I don't want to wait to find out."

Was this just a polite way of getting around to telling her to take Amy and leave? That he'd decided he didn't want any part of either of them after all, regardless of what the DNA test might show?

"What does that mean—you don't want to wait to find out?" Karis asked quietly.

"Look, I know this is fast. Crazy fast. Again. But there's something here, with the three of us. With you and me. With Amy and me. She might not be my flesh and blood, but for five weeks I thought she was and now...well, now it doesn't matter whether some test says she is or not, she still *feels* like she's mine. I still feel about her the way I did when I thought she was. So I don't care what the test shows. I'm on her birth certificate as her father and I want to *be* her father."

Is he just kicking me out?

"That's nice," Karis said softly, her stress increasing by the minute.

"I'm not just being *nice*," Luke said. "I'm telling you that I had a revelation and part of it was about Amy. But an even bigger part of it was about you. And me and the way I feel about you and what I want for us. I want us to be together. You and I. You and I and Amy. I want to see if we can't make what's going on here really work. For the long run."

"What's going on here…" Karis repeated.

"I thought you were just another Lea when you showed up on my doorstep. But the more I've gotten to know you and what kind of person you are, the more I know that you aren't anything like Lea. And today, when it hit me that coming home to you, to Amy, felt like where I was meant to be, that it sure as hell was where I *wanted* to be, I knew that Lea isn't in any of this. This is about you and me, about Amy. This is about what we are to each other here and now. What we can be to each other from this point on. And I want us to be every-thing to each other. I want us to be a family."

The shiver that went through Karis had nothing to do with temperature or with tension. It was a little shiver of delight. And for one brief moment all she thought was that he wanted her. Luke wanted her! As much as she wanted him. He wanted Amy. He wanted them to stay together. This past week had been such a relief from the fear and flux she'd lived under for the six weeks before it, and it didn't have to

end. She could have a place with Luke, in his
life, the way she had this week. The way she
had last night. She could belong to him, to everything that went with him, maybe even to that
other portion of her own family.

Then reality crept in and she remembered
there were complications with that other
portion of her family. She wasn't free to just
shed the past the way Luke was, to forget all
about it and start over. There was something
else that he didn't even know about.

And that was when she said, "Wait…" in a
voice so low it was almost inaudible.

"Wait?" he repeated with a laugh. "Wait for
what?"

"I need to tell you one more thing."

Oh, she hated that that was all it took for him
to pull back. Only slightly, only enough to make
him sit up straighter, only enough to make his
hands a fraction less firm in the way they were
holding hers. But enough to see, to feel, to
know there was still a part of him that was leery
in spite of the fact that he'd said his concerns
didn't exist anymore.

"What don't I know?" he asked.

Lord, how she didn't want to say what she
had to say. How she didn't want him to think
badly of her again.

Maybe she should have told him this from the start, too. Maybe she should never have kept anything a secret.

But she had.

And she couldn't any longer.

So she gave him a small, weak, guilty smile and said, "There was another reason I came to Northbridge besides Amy."

He drew back a little more. Now her hands were only lying in his. He wasn't holding them at all.

"Uh-huh…" he said.

Karis sighed. "This is hard. I hate it. But I don't know how you'll feel about this and before you say anything else along the lines you were headed—"

"Just tell me."

There was a sharper edge to his tone. A sharper edge of suspicion that cut her to the quick with how fast it could come alive in him again.

Karis took her hands out of his and folded them in her lap because she didn't think she could bear it when he pulled away completely, as she thought he was on the verge of doing.

She squared her shoulders slightly and said, "I own the house up the hill."

Luke's brows dipped together over eyes that had turned a darker, stormier green in the last few minutes. "What do you mean you own the house up the hill? The Pratts' house?"

Karis nodded.

"That's your other iron in the fire," he said as if light had just dawned.

"Yes."

His frown deepened even more. "But how?"

"It's convoluted. You know that my father and the other Pratts' mother were never divorced. That's why he and my mother were never married. I told you that he had a will that left everything he owned to me when he died. Well, when I went through his things, I found a letter from an attorney here named Harvey Drake—"

"He's the Pratts' lawyer. He's the lawyer for most people around here."

"Well, the letter he sent my father informed him that Loretta Pratt had died. And that because they were still technically married at the time of her death, because my father's name was still on her house and she *hadn't* left a will that said otherwise, my father had become the owner of the place. Which, according to the lawyer, was really all she had except for furniture and personal belongings."

"The Pratts had been taking care of their mother financially for a while. I'm sure the house *was* all she had. But I can't believe they didn't know this."

"In the letter Harvey Drake said that the family didn't know my father's name had been added to the title when he'd married Loretta—apparently Mr. Drake had handled that and so decided that confidentiality for that at least was owed my father. He said that he'd advised Loretta repeatedly to have the title changed, that the house had been built by her grandfather and should only be in her name or the names of her children, not in the name of the man who had deserted them all. But she'd never done it. So without a will, the house just automatically went to Dad when she died. The lawyer urged my father to do the right thing and just sign the house over to his other children. But when I called Mr. Drake he said my father hadn't done that. And that yes, if my father had a will that left everything of his to me, that included the house here."

After a moment during which Luke looked as if he was letting that sink in, he said, "So you own their house."

"I do."

He got up from the chair and went to the farthest corner of the kitchen, where he turned to face her again, leaning his hips against the edge of the countertop, grabbing on to it with both hands as if he needed some anchoring and staring at her in disbelief as he repeated, "You own the Pratts' house."

"And it's the only asset I have in the world," Karis said, again her voice quiet.

"So you're going to take it from them? Throw them out?"

"No," she said quickly, firmly. "But what I need to do is mortgage it for the rest of the money to pay off what Lea took. It won't change anything for the Pratts. I won't borrow any more than I have to and that's a lot less than the place is worth. They'll be able to go on living there and then when I get the mortgage paid off I'll sign the title over to them free and clear. But until then—"

"The house they all think belongs to them really belongs to you and you're going to take out a loan on it. And if you don't pay the payments, they'll have to."

So he was jumping right to the worst-case scenario.

"I won't *not* pay the payments," she said forcefully. "I won't let them lose their house. I just have to use it as collateral—"

"And they don't know," he said, as if even as she spoke the wheels of his mind were spinning ahead.

"I need to tell them," she admitted.

"But you haven't. You've been friendly toward them. You've lured them in with Amy—"

"I didn't lure them in," Karis said, her voice gaining strength. "Amy is a separate issue and she's their niece no matter what else is going on."

"You were still getting them warmed up before you struck," he accused.

Karis shook her head firmly and fought instant, hot tears. "No, I wasn't. And I'm not *striking*."

"You didn't go right in there the first day and let them know where they stood. You pretended all you wanted was to tell them their father was dead. And you didn't use any of the other opportunities you've had, either. But you've opened the door for them to see how cute Amy is. You've had them hold her and play with her. You've gotten in closer and closer that way—"

"No! That isn't how it's been. I haven't told them, because I hate that things are how they are. I haven't told them, because it's ugly and awful and I don't want to do what I have to do. I haven't told them, because no matter how they think they feel about our father, it stinks that he made a will and even left them out of that, and that now I have to be the one to deliver that message, too. I haven't told them, because I wish I didn't have to at all and so I've dragged my feet about it. I haven't told them, because maybe it would be nice to have brothers and sisters—even half brothers and sisters—who don't think I'm no better than their other half sister who stole from them. I haven't told them, because maybe it would be nice to have what you have here with your family and what they have with each other, instead of what I don't have."

And she hadn't wanted to cry, but there she was, crying anyway.

"An Kras?" Amy said, sounding scared, her own little voice wobbly with the threat of tears, too.

"It's all right, sweetheart, it's all right," Karis said soothingly, swiping at the moisture on her face and fighting to keep more tears from falling as she stood and took Amy out of the high chair.

Only when she was hugging the baby to her did she look at Luke again. His expression was dark and unreadable now, but Karis couldn't seem to stop herself from going on.

"I know. You figure I just fooled you. That I'm Lea all over again and you were dumb to believe even for a split second that I'm not. But it isn't true and somewhere down the road you'll see that. Nobody will get hurt, because I'll make sure of it. But until then I guess you'll just have to think whatever you want to think."

Then she took Amy and walked out of the kitchen.

And all the way through the living room and up the stairs to the nursery, there was a small part of her that wondered—hoped—Luke would follow her. That he would say it was all right. That everything could be okay.

But he didn't.

Instead, a few minutes after she got to the nursery, she heard the front door open and close.

And when she looked out the second-floor window she saw Luke headed up the hill.

No doubt for the Pratts' house.

To warn them about her.

Chapter Thirteen

"It wouldn't have worked out anyway," Karis said as she bathed Amy just after Luke left the house.

Amy was far more interested in her rubber frog than in what Karis was saying, but Karis was too distraught not to go on as if she had a rapt audience.

"I don't want a life on the coattails of what Lea did here. With a lot of people who dislike me by association. Who won't ever trust me. What kind of future could there be for me in that? With Luke and everyone else always on the lookout, always ready to jump to the worst conclusion."

"Foggy?"

"Yes, that's froggy," Karis confirmed before going on basically talking to herself. "Sure, I watched them all from the sidelines and I was jealous and I wanted what they have here. But now I know that can't happen where Lea has already done damage. I should be glad that my eyes were opened before this went any further."

"Eye," Amy repeated, pointing to hers with a bubbly hand.

"Yes, that's your eye," Karis said, feeling her own eyes stinging again as she couldn't help thinking about Luke and that one fleeting moment when she'd entertained the idea that she really might be able to have him. To be with him. Not to have the previous night be the only one she was ever allowed.

"But things are the way they are," she said in a bumpy voice. "And probably he's going to come back here any minute with the Pratts and they'll run me out of town."

Only after she'd said that did it actually dawn on her that that could well be the case. Surely none of them would want her around. Luke wouldn't want her living in his house. The other Pratts would most likely shun her. And in a community as close-knit as Northbridge she'd be persona non grata everywhere.

But Luke had decided that he *did* want Amy...

"What if he sticks with that and just banishes me?" she whispered to herself.

In the three scenarios she'd envisioned when she'd brought Amy to Northbridge—Luke slamming the door in her face; Luke taking Amy temporarily until he found out he *wasn't* her father; Luke actually being Amy's dad—never had Karis imagined that she would lose Amy altogether.

Even if Luke proved to be Amy's father and wanted to keep her, Karis had made up her mind in advance that she would move to Billings or somewhere else close by. She would try to get Luke to agree to share custody but, failing that, she would make sure she was a part of Amy's life—the aunt Amy saw every weekend, every holiday, every vacation, every chance Karis got. The aunt who would always be there for her no matter what.

Not in any of those scenarios had Karis considered that she might be completely kept away from Amy.

Now it occurred to her that, if Luke wanted Amy but refused to have anything to do with her, losing Amy was exactly what could happen.

And she couldn't let it.

Panic shot through her despair and, without finishing Amy's bath, she took the baby out of the tub and wrapped a towel around her.

"We have to get out of here," she told Amy as she rushed to the nursery.

She'd never diapered and dressed the baby so fast. Then she set Amy in the crib and, while Amy watched, Karis began to stuff everything she could into the diaper bag and the cardboard box that had held Amy's things when she'd brought her here.

Once she had it all ready to go—and without any thought of her own belongings—Karis ran to Luke's room, intent on only one thing.

She had to find her car keys.

"Dow," Amy demanded from the nursery, not happy to have been left there.

"I know. I'll be right back," Karis called to her as she steadfastly refused to look at the bed where she and Luke had made love all night. She tried not to recall how fantastic it had been, how she'd wanted nothing but to stay like that with him forever.

She tried not to notice that the scent of his cologne still lingered on his suit pants as she went through his pockets. Tried not to think about how those slacks had come off. About what had waited for her beneath them. About the body she knew she was never going to stop craving.

She tried not to even look at the condoms that were in the nightstand drawer she rifled through, or think about how many of them they'd used, how many more she would have liked the chance to use.

She tried to focus only on the jeopardy she was in as she opened dresser drawers and images of Luke wearing the clothes she came upon flashed through her mind to torture her with more longing for him.

"What are you looking for?"

Karis jumped.

Luke was standing in his bedroom doorway, leaning one shoulder against the frame.

She hadn't heard him come back, let alone get all the way to where he could catch her searching his things.

But she stood up straight, faced him and said, "I need my car keys. I'll take Amy and go."

Then she held her breath, hoping his feelings for Amy had taken yet another turn so that he wouldn't insist on keeping the baby and might actually let them both leave.

For a moment he didn't do or say anything. He merely stood there, staring at her, his expression even more indecipherable than it had been in the kitchen earlier.

Then he put his hand in his jeans pocket and pulled out her key ring. "I have your keys. But right now you need to come downstairs with me."

It was Karis's turn to be suspicious. "Why?"

"You just do," he said, putting the keys back in his pocket before he pushed off the door frame and left as silently as he'd arrived.

Karis didn't know what to do but follow him. First she went to the nursery to get Amy, who was letting it be known she didn't like being left there.

When Karis got Amy downstairs, though, she didn't find only Luke waiting in the living room. Mara, Neily, Cam and Taylor were there, too.

It was daunting to face them all, especially not knowing why they were there or what was going to happen, and so Karis stopped in the archway from the entry rather than going completely into the living room.

"You can come in and sit down. Nobody will bite," Luke said.

"I'm fine," Karis answered, half-wondering if she should make a run for it.

"Come on. It's okay," Mara said in a voice that lacked the hostility Karis thought it would have.

But still Karis stayed planted on the outskirts. "I'm okay. Just say…or do…whatever you're all here for."

For the first time since she'd told Luke about inheriting the Pratts' house, he cracked a small smile. "What do you think? That we're going to stone you or something?"

"Maybe," she said, holding Amy with a protective hand on the baby's back.

"It's been at least two weeks since we've stoned anybody," Taylor joked.

Okay, so maybe the tone wasn't quite as bad as she'd expected. But still Karis had no idea what was going on and didn't budge. Or say anything. She just waited for them to tell her what was going on, paying no attention to Amy playing with her hair.

Luckily Luke didn't waste any more time.

"I told them about the house," he said then. "We've talked it over—on the phone to Jon, Boone and Scott, too—and this is what we've come up with. Between your seven half siblings and me, we can raise the rest of the money you need. So we'll float the loan. In return for that, what we want you to do is put your name and theirs on the title so you all own the place equally."

"Seriously?" Karis asked, glancing from one

face to another, because she couldn't believe what she was hearing.

"Seriously," Neily confirmed. "Luke vouched for you and this seemed fair to everyone. Well, there isn't anything in it for Luke, but he said he wants to help."

"We had no idea the house wasn't in Mom's name alone, that we all hadn't inherited it as a matter of course," Mara added. "This way we get the house back and you get a share in it plus the money you need."

"Money that everyone will have returned to them through the payments you make," Luke contributed before going on. "I also called my brother Ben. He mentioned last night at the wedding that he's looking for someone to do bookwork, paperwork, and to fill out and file insurance and social security forms for the kids in his school. It's a full-time job with a full-time salary, but you'd only need to be at the school a couple of hours a day. Most of it can be done at home, so you wouldn't have to leave Amy. And when you do need to go in, my mom would be willing to babysit if I'm on duty."

Karis suddenly *needed* to sit down. She took the desk chair just inside the archway and sat, situating Amy on her lap. There was a set of coasters on the desk that grabbed the baby's attention, oblivious to what was happening around her.

Mara spoke up again. "Luke told us about the will and how the house became yours and how much you hated to let us know. We won't pretend that we were thrilled with the news but we don't hold it against you. We think that Mom just never lost hope that...*Dad* would come back to her and that's why she didn't take his name off the house. Luke also told us that it wasn't as if you had a great father in our mutual parent, either, and the truth is, we all talked about it and about you and Amy, and we decided Luke was right about something else he said—about how you and Amy both deserve to be seen in your own right and not judged by anything Lea or anyone else did. So maybe we can go from here and really get to know each other and put everything behind us."

"Luke convinced you of all that?" Karis asked quietly.

"We were thinking that maybe he should have been a hostage negotiator or a victim's advocate instead of a cop," Neily teased him.

Karis looked at Luke, too stunned to know what to say to him.

"It was a long walk up the hill," he said, as if that were an explanation.

"It must have been."

For a moment their eyes locked and the other Pratts must have seen something passing between them because Mara said, "We can work out the details later. Maybe we should leave the two of you to talk?"

"That might be a good idea," Luke answered without breaking eye contact with Karis.

"And maybe we could take Amy up the hill with us to get her out of your hair for a little while," Neily suggested.

Karis had a moment's hesitation as this all seemed too good to be true, and fleetingly she thought it was possible that this whole thing had only been a plot to get Amy away from her.

But rational thought prevailed and she realized that was far-fetched so she conceded.

Karis took Amy into the entry, followed behind by the other Pratts, with Luke bringing up the rear.

As Karis put on the baby's coat and bundled her into the stroller, Mara said, "We also want you to know that you and Amy can move into the house with us if you want. It's big and there are empty rooms, since not all of us live there anymore."

"Thanks," Karis said, surprised by that offer, too.

Then it occurred to her that she'd been so

stunned by everything that she really hadn't said much of anything, so once Amy was settled, she let her gaze take in her half siblings and said, "I'm sorry this all happened and I can't begin to put into words how grateful I am that you're taking it like this and helping out, too. But honestly, if you don't feel comfortable with any of it—"

"It's one of the advantages of a big family," Cam said. "Everybody pitches in when one of us is in trouble."

Karis's eyes filled with tears yet again, not only for what was being done for her, not only for being included as one of the Pratt family, but also because it had come from Cam. Cam, who had seemed like her harshest critic when she'd first met the other Pratts, and who had also been more standoffish than the rest.

The four other Pratts took Amy and left then, and suddenly Karis was alone with Luke.

He'd remained in the background while she'd gotten Amy ready to go and now he was the one in the connecting archway between the entry and living room, while Karis was near the foot of the stairs.

She turned to face him, taking in the sight of him once more leaning one shoulder to the edge of the arch, his arms crossed over his broad chest again, watching her.

"So," she said, at a loss for more to say.

"So," he countered, tossing the proverbial ball back in her court.

"You were busy in the last hour or so."

"I was."

"I guess I'm not sure why," she ventured.

She saw his chest rise and fall with a deep breath before he shrugged. "I'll admit I had a minute when you told me about the house that I thought the worst. When I thought, *here we go again.* But then you had that meltdown over the reasons you *hadn't* told the other Pratts about their house and I saw all over again how different you are from Lea. All those things you care about—hurting people you don't even know by telling them that their father ignored them in death the same way he'd ignored them in life, not wanting to be the one to deliver that message—I think the only thing Lea would have done was rub her hands together in greedy glee over how much she could make. I think she would have tried ransoming the place back to the other Pratts. I know she wouldn't have planned to borrow the money somewhere else to keep them from being affected. So that was what I told them when I went up there. I said that yes, you own their house and hadn't told them, but that you could have had a whole lot worse up your sleeve. And we all agreed that Lea would have."

"But in the kitchen you—"

"I know. I'm sorry. I shouldn't have accused you of using Amy to lure them in. I know that isn't something you'd do either. I just had this Lea flashback and it temporarily blinded me and I struck out at you."

"Oh."

Luke frowned. "That was an ominous *oh*."

"The Lea-flashback blindness—that reminds me of why I didn't want anything to happen between us from the start. And what I was thinking again after you left this morning."

"You've lost me."

"I don't want to carry that stigma."

"The Lea stigma," he said.

"I don't want to be always worrying that the slightest thing will bring out the suspicions again. That I'll be instantly condemned because—"

"Because I'm an idiot?"

"I'm not saying that. You have good reason—"

"*I'm* saying I was an idiot. I came in here this morning telling you that I know you aren't your sister and then I threw it out the window a second later."

"Well, yeah," Karis allowed.

Luke pulled away from the wall and moved a few steps toward her. "How about we agree to meet halfway on this. I said I was sorry for doubting you and suspecting the worst of you and I promise that I will never—*never again*—let myself forget that you are a totally different person than your sister was."

"And my halfway?"

"You'll admit that it's a pretty big bombshell to drop that you own a house that belongs to other people and kept it quiet until now."

"I had reasons."

"I know you did. And I understand that. I'm just saying that if ever there was a flashbulb big enough to temporarily blind somebody, it was that."

Karis didn't have to think long to concede. "Okay, that's true. But—"

"But nothing. I come halfway and swear that from this minute on you are disconnected in my head from your sister and any failings she had and anything she ever did. And you come halfway and swear there aren't any more secrets to throw out at me. And then we go on."

So she just had to trust that he would be as good as his word.

A part of Karis was afraid to do that. She

worried that he couldn't do what he was swearing he would. That there was no escaping the ashes left from Lea burning through his life.

But then it occurred to her that he'd taken more than a small step in proving he could see her for herself. He'd convinced his lifelong friends to take a risk on her. To let her into their lives. He was betting money of his own on her. *He* was trusting *her.* How could she not trust him in return?

Especially when she wanted to. When she wanted to believe he saw her for herself. When she wanted to go back to the brief moment of hope that she'd had earlier that she might actually be able to have a future with him.

"What do we go on to?" she asked in a quiet voice, referring to the last thing he'd said to her.

"To what I was talking about when I first came in this morning. To you and me. To you and me and Amy being a family."

"Does that mean you don't want Amy and me to move up the hill with the real Pratts?"

He took another few steps toward her, ending up standing directly in front of her without touching her.

"That's what it means. And how about I make you a *real* Walker so we can just call them the Pratts?"

Karis's smile was involuntary. "I'm getting a loan, a job *and* a husband, all in one morning?"

"And a daughter—don't forget that I come with a kid."

Her smile got bigger. "Oh, yeah, I forgot."

"So what do you say?" he asked, his tone softer, more intimate, and tinged with a vulnerability that surprised and touched her.

"I say Karis Walker has a nice ring to it."

This time it was his smile that seemed spontaneous as he wrapped her in his arms and pulled her to him, kissing away any lingering doubts she might have had, because just having his mouth on hers again reminded her of how much she cared for this man, how much she yearned for him.

So much that suddenly nothing was as important as just being there against that body she craved, as just having her breasts pressed to his massive chest, as losing herself in the kiss that needed no urging to deepen.

Mouths were open wide and tongues held nothing back as hands plunged into frenzied searching and seeking, arousing and tantalizing.

Somehow they made it up the stairs without losing contact, shedding shoes and socks and Luke's thick sweater that Karis had wanted to take off him hours ago.

His bedroom was still in disarray after her search but that didn't matter. In fact it aided the cause since his nightstand drawer offered its contents before Luke nudged it closed with his thigh.

Mouths clung together as he made quick work of the buttons of her sweater and tossed it aside along with her bra. His hands reached her already straining, engorged breasts as hers unzipped his jeans and slid them down with his boxers.

Her jeans and panties were the last to go and then they reclaimed the bed and each other in a turbulent coming together of bodies that seemed starved for each other. Bodies that meshed and mingled and melded into one glorious joining of his with hers, sending sky-rockets into flight and taking them both along for the ride, higher and higher. The climactic explosion truly sealed their union of lives and spirits so powerfully that when it was over Karis wasn't even sure how they'd gotten from the entryway to where they ended up.

She had no complaints, though, lying all tangled with Luke, who stroked her hair and kissed her eyes, her nose, her cheeks and then her mouth again before he said, "I love you, Karis."

That made her smile instantaneously once more. "I love you, too. So much."

"Everything was worth it if it had to happen to bring us to this. Together," he said then.

"For me, too. Although I might not have believed it en route."

"And everything will be all right from now."

"I know."

She did know. How could it be anything but all right when, in one fell swoop, she was getting a home, a family, an extended family and—most importantly—Luke.

"Does this mean I can have my car keys back?" she joked, to keep herself from crying yet again today.

"Sure, but why don't you wait until I put the jeans back on to root around in the pocket for them? When I watched you doing that earlier with the suit pants I was wishing I was in them."

That made her laugh.

He tightened his arms around her and settled his chin on the top of her head. "I really do love you," he said again, his voice slower, softer.

Karis kissed his chest and closed her eyes, feeling him relaxing and knowing he was drifting off.

She didn't want to sleep, though. She just wanted to lie there awake and soak in all that had happened and how so much bad had turned into so much good in such a short amount of time.

And all because of Luke.

That was when it struck her that in a life that had hardly been full of accomplishments, Lea had managed two very big ones.

Amy.

And bringing Karis and Luke together.

Luke, who had made a dream come true of the nightmares Lea had caused for them both.

And while that might not have made up for the damage Lea had done to so many people, it made up for a whole lot for Karis.

Because no matter where it had come from, now she would have a better future than she'd ever hoped for. With this man who felt like the other half of her being. This man she would have never found without her sister.

And for that she had to be grateful.

A million times over.

Grateful.

Content.

Complete.

And oh so happy.

It was a happiness that Luke shared with Karis. A happiness that wasn't diminished, even five weeks later when he learned that Amy wasn't his biological daughter.

Because now that he had Karis and Amy in his life, marriage and adoption would make them his family.

His real, true family.

For all time.

* * * * *

Don't miss the next installment of
Victoria Pade's popular
NORTHBRIDGE NUPTIALS
when you'll find out who Celeste really is!
Look for HOMETOWN CINDERELLA
in January 2007
only from Silhouette Special Edition.

*Experience entertaining women's fiction
about rediscovery and reconnection—warm,
compelling stories that are relevant
for every woman who has wondered
"What's next?" in their lives.
After all, there's the life you planned.
And there's what comes next.*

*Turn the page for a sneak preview
of a new book from Harlequin NEXT.*

*CONFESSIONS OF A NOT-SO-DEAD LIBIDO
by Peggy Webb*

*On sale November 2006,
wherever books are sold.*

My husband could see beauty in a mud puddle. Literally. "Look at that, Louise," he'd say after a heavy spring rain. "Have you ever seen so many amazing colors in mud?"

I'd look and see nothing except brown, but he'd pick up a stick and swirl the mud till the colors of the earth emerged, and all of a sudden I'd see the world through his eyes—extraordinary instead of mundane.

Roy was my mirror to life. Four years ago when he died, it cracked wide open, and I've been living a smashed-up, sleepwalking life ever since.

If he were here on this balmy August night I'd be sailing with him instead of baking cheese straws in preparation for Tuesday-night quilting club with Patsy. I'd be striving for sex appeal in Bermuda shorts and bare-toed sandals instead of opting for comfort in walking shoes and a twill skirt with enough elastic around the waist to make allowances for two helpings of lemon-cream pie.

Not that I mind Patsy. Just the opposite. I love her. She's the only person besides Roy who creates wonder wherever she goes. (She creates mayhem, too, but we won't get into that.) She's my mirror now, as well as my compass.

Of course, I have my daughter, Diana, but I refuse to be the kind of mother who defines herself through her children. Besides, she has her own life now, a husband and a baby on the way.

I slide the last cheese straws into the oven and then go into my office and open e-mail.

From: "Miss Sass" <patsyleslie@hotmail.com>
To: "The Lady" <louisejernigan@yahoo.com>
Sent: Tuesday, August 15, 6:00 PM
Subject: Dangerous Tonight
Hey Lady,

I'm feeling dangerous tonight. Hot to trot, if you know what I mean. Or can you even remember? ☺ Look out, bridge club, here I come. I'm liable to end up dancing on the tables instead of

bidding three spades. Whose turn is it to drive, anyhow? Mine or thine?
XOXOX
Patsy
P.S. Lord, how did we end up in a club with no men?

This e-mail is typical "Patsy." She's the only person I know who makes me laugh all the time. I guess that's why I e-mail her about ten times a day. She lives right next door, but e-mail satisfies my urge to be instantly and constantly in touch with her without having to interrupt the flow of my life. Sometimes we even save the good stuff for e-mail.

From: "The Lady" <louisejernigan@yahoo.com>
To: "Miss Sass" <patsyleslie@hotmail.com>
Sent: Tuesday, August 15, 6:10 PM
Subject: Re: Dangerous Tonight
So, what else is new, Miss Sass? You're always dangerous. If you had a weapon, you'd be lethal. ☺
Hugs,
Louise
P.S. What's this about men? I thought you said your libido was dead?

I press Send then wait. Her reply is almost instantaneous.

From: "Miss Sass" <patsyleslie@hotmail.com>
To: "The Lady" <louisejernigan@yahoo.com>
Sent: Tuesday, August 15, 6:12 PM
Subject: Re: Dangerous Tonight
Ha! If I had a *brain* I'd be lethal.
And I said my libido was in hibernation, not DEAD!
Jeez, Louise!!!!!
P

Patsy loves to have the last word, so I shut off my computer.

* * * * *

*Want to find out what happens
to their friendship
when Patsy and Louise both find
the perfect man?*

Don't miss
CONFESSIONS OF A NOT-SO-DEAD LIBIDO
by Peggy Webb,
coming to Harlequin NEXT
in November 2006.

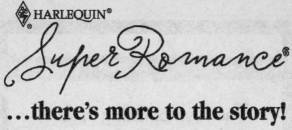
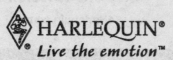

Harlequin® Historical
Historical Romantic Adventure!

*Imagine a time of chivalrous
knights and unconventional ladies,
roguish rakes and impetuous
heiresses, rugged cowboys
and spirited frontierswomen—
these rich and vivid tales will
capture your imagination!*

*Harlequin Historical . . .
they're too good to miss!*

SILHOUETTE *Romance*

Escape to a place where a kiss is still a kiss...

Feel the breathless connection...

Fall in love as though it were
the very first time...

Experience the power of love!

Come to where favorite authors—such as

Diana Palmer, Judy Christenberry, Marie Ferrarella

and many more—deliver modern fairy tale
romances and genuine emotion,
time after time after time....

Silhouette Romance—
from today to forever.

Silhouette®

Live the possibilities